I0628587

IT STARTED WITH BESSE

The Tanners, Book 3

Pamela Ann Cleverly

This book is a work of fiction. Names, characters, organizations, companies, and incidents are products of the author's imagination or, if real, are used fictitiously. Any resemblance to actual persons, living or dead, or to events, is entirely coincidental.

All Rights reserved. No part of this book may be reproduced or transmitted in any form or by any means, electronic or mechanical, including photocopying, recording, or by any information storage and retrieval system, without the written permission of the author.

CLEVER INK, LLC,
Mentor, OH

Copyright © 2021 Pamela Ann Cleverly
All rights reserved.

ISBN-13: 978-0-9970522-4-4
Library of Congress Control Number: 2021903752

ALSO BY PAMELA ANN CLEVERLY

The Tanners Series

In The Shadow Of The Lighthouse, Book 1

A Beacon In The Dark, Book 2

*This book is dedicated to my amazing critique partners,
my beta readers who convinced me the book was ready to
publish and my family who never quit pushing me forward.*

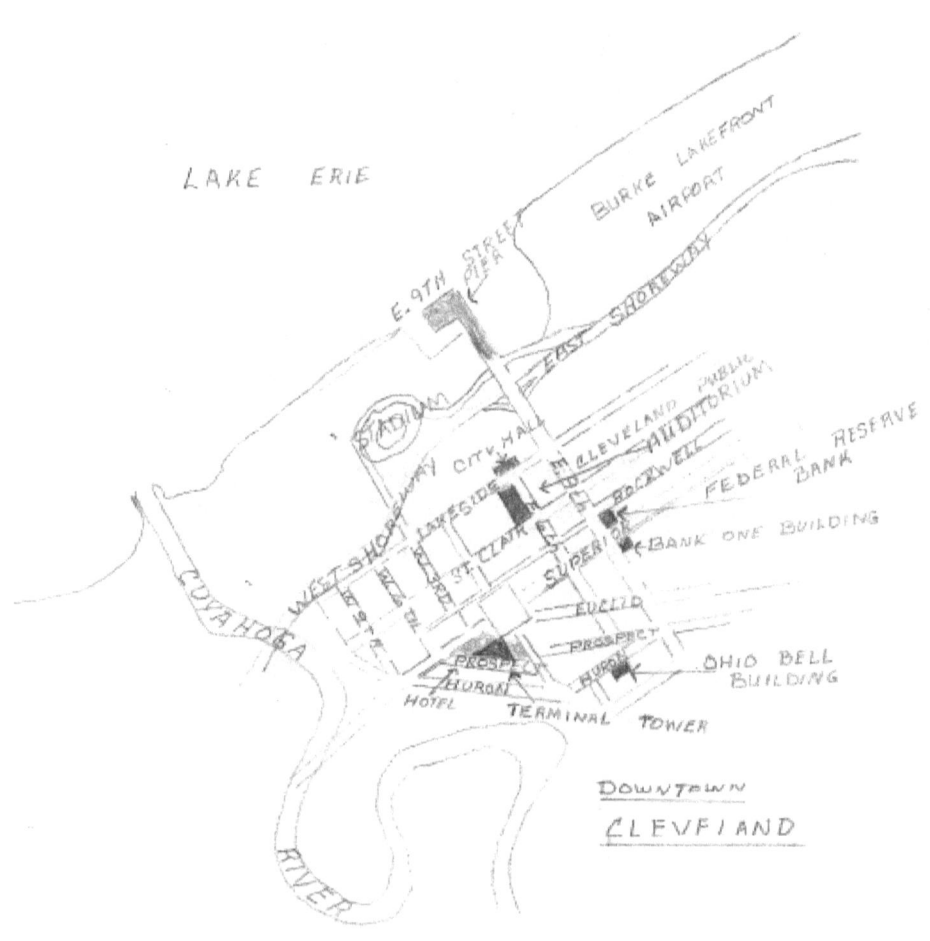

LAKE ERIE

DOWNTOWN
CLEVELAND

1

Sunday, April 21, 1991
Cleveland, Ohio
Terminal Tower, 10:00 A.M.

Five hundred watts of light suddenly filled the hallway. Morgan blinked. Her eyes took a moment to adjust. She smoothed the front of her royal-blue wool suit jacket. The cameraman raised his left arm, fingers spread for the countdown. Five, four, three, two, one.

"Hello. I'm Morgan Tanner, and this is another segment in the series, *Secrets of Cleveland.* Beyond this door is a world few people know exists. Yet it's in the most famous building in Cleveland and back in the early 1920s the second tallest skyscraper in the United States. The Greenbrier Suite gives us insight into the opulent lifestyle of two brothers who changed the face of a city forever."

Morgan turned the brass doorknob. She pushed open the door a few inches, then hesitated. She wanted to create a sense of mystery of what lay beyond. Mystery and suspense drove ratings up. If she were to keep her pet project on the air, those ratings would need to skyrocket into the stratosphere. *Secrets* had been a hard sell to the station bigwigs and sponsors. There was much more to her than the fluff jobs handed down by the station manager. This segment needed to be better than good––it needed to get noticed.

Morgan stepped to the side and glanced over her left shoulder, never taking her eyes off the camera lens. "We're about to enter the brothers' apartment and join Naomi Franklin here on the fourteenth floor of the magnificent Terminal Tower. Many of you may not even know the name Van Sweringen. There are no roads or streets named after the brothers. Oris and Mantis never married and lived a very private life behind these walls, as well as their English Tudor style mansion in Shaker Heights and later in their 54-room manor, Roundwood in Hunting Valley."

Morgan used her free right arm to push the door back against the wall. She tilted her head just enough so her hair would fall obstructing her eyes from the camera's view. She just needed a second to make sure Naomi, the building concierge, was in place as previously directed. She gave Naomi a wink and then focused her full attention on the camera. Raising the microphone closer to her lips she backed a few steps into the room beyond. She beckoned with her hand for her audience to follow.

She lowered her chin a tad and her voice an octave for a mysterious effect. "Follow me back in time and find out what finally derailed the Van Sweringen brothers' fast train into Cleveland's future."

Two hours later Morgan, Naomi and her cameraman, Jerry Kaminski, stood outside the door to the Greenbrier apartment. Jerry bent his middle-aged gut close to the carrying cases on the floor. He placed the heavy camera, battery pack and light into their compartments.

"I think this wraps it up," Morgan said. She shook Naomi's hand. "Thank you for your help. We have a lot of great footage. I'll call you if I have any questions during editing." She knew she would. She always had additional questions. She'd only been a television reporter for six months and the camera still intimidated her, sending her into moments of brain-freeze when she should be totally focused on the subject at hand.

A vibration tickled at Morgan's waist. She tilted the small black box attached to her belt so she could read the phone number appearing across the screen. Since becoming WJW TV8's newest reporter, Morgan had gotten used to pagers being a permanent part of her wardrobe. For the past year, she'd been tied by the invisible umbilical cord to the newsroom, either by way of the mobile phones mounted in the truck and her car, or the cumbersome bag phone. Sam McIntire, the station manager, had presented her with the latest Motorola mobile phone with the flourish he might bestow on an Emmy winner. Weighing in at four pounds, the large case was just one more thing to sling over her shoulder along with her tote bag and briefcase. The most frustrating part was how it always seemed out of range of the few cell towers. For this shoot, she'd left it in the truck.

"Naomi, is there a phone I can use to call the station?" Morgan asked.

"Sure, I have to call home anyway. I'm running later than I expected." Naomi glanced down at Morgan's left hand. "Sunday dinner at the in-laws. We usually go right from church but since I had this interview with you we agreed to meet them later. My husband's a great guy, but I can't say the same for his mother." She raised her shoulders with an expression that said *Oh well. I'm stuck with her.* "I don't see a ring, so I assume you don't have to deal with a mother-in-law."

Morgan's pager went off for the second time. Happy to have an excuse not to answer Naomi's probe into her private life, Morgan glanced down at the screen. "It's the restricted line in the newsroom. Must be important. You'd better lead me to the phone."

A few minutes later Morgan sat on the edge of the desk in a small, windowless room that served as an office. The buttercup walls were probably an attempt at making what had obviously been a storage closet somewhat cheerful. Morgan aligned the black pushbutton phone in front of her and punched in the number for the newsroom.

Morgan slipped off her right shoe while listening to the ringing. She reached down to rub her sore foot. She'd been stupid to wear new heels on an assignment requiring a lot of walking. All she wanted was to go home, get into a pair of sweats and start the new John Grisham book, *The Firm.* She loved books full of plot twists and suspense. The books were a far cry from her life. Although her world as a reporter was interesting, it certainly had no suspense. Any further thoughts on her aching feet and books ended when the station manager answered the restricted line. "Yeah?"

"It's me, Sam."

"Listen, Morgan. We have a situation," he said in a rushed tone she knew only too well. He had a problem and it was about to be dumped on her.

"Yeah, Boss, we're on our way out. Be back in the studio within the hour."

Morgan put her free hand over her ear to hear Sam better. The few words she picked up didn't make sense. She made a cutting gesture so Naomi and Jerry would stop talking. "I'm sorry, could you repeat that? I don't think I heard you correctly." She hopped down off the desk and slipped her foot back into her shoe as an icy veil of fear enveloped her.

"I said, there's been some sort of explosion at the Davis-Besse Nuclear Power Plant near Port Clinton. The sirens have gone off and they're evacuating the area."

Morgan's heart pounded in a siege of panic. "Are you sure? When did this happen? What about radiation?" She paused long enough to fill her lungs. "What do you want us to do?"

"I'm sure. I want you and Jerry to get back here immediately."

She ended the call, reminding herself to breathe. Morgan hoped the others didn't see the panic in her eyes or hear the jackhammer in her chest.

Jerry entered the office from the hallway. Naomi leaned against the doorframe.

"I know that look, Morgan." Jerry moved to her side. "I'd bet money on the fact we're not finished for the day. What's up?"

Naomi crossed her arms over her chest. "Come on, how bad can it be? Do they want footage on the Terminal Tower or the train station? I'd be happy to call off on my mother-in-law's Sunday dinner."

"There's been an explosion at the Davis-Besse Nuclear Power Plant." The room began to spin. Morgan grabbed the edge of the desk. "Sirens. Radiation. Evacuating." She forced air into her lungs––in––out––in––out. Fainting wasn't an option. "My family's there," Morgan was able to get the words out in a hoarse voice.

Jerry put his arm around Morgan's shoulders for support. "Relax. Breathe deep. I'm sure they're fine."

Naomi moved a few steps into the room. "I don't understand."

"Most of Morgan's family lives within spitting distance of Davis-Besse. Morgan, her brother Michael, and their mother are the only ones who live in the Cleveland area."

"I remember the Three Mile Island accident in '79. I did a report on it for school. It was a partial meltdown of reactor number 2, near Harrisburg, Pennsylvania. There was a radiation leak. That was really bad," said Naomi while scrunching her face as if trying to remember more.

"You're not helping, Naomi," Jerry said with a *shut the hell up* look.

Morgan pushed free of Jerry's arm. "I have to do something. I have to help my family. But Sam wants us to head back to the station."

"I have an idea." Jerry walked back to where he'd left his equipment in the hallway. "Naomi, can you get us to the observation deck?"

"The observation deck is closed to the public, but I have the keys. I thought you and Morgan had to get back to the station."

"The station manager just wants to round up the troops and have us all sitting around as the story unfolds. Wait and see if it's real or just a lot of hype. Believe me, we have some time."

Morgan wiped beads of sweat from her forehead with the back of her hand. "This *is* a real story!"

"Trust me. This is better than sitting around waiting for Sam to tell us what to do," Jerry said as he hefted his camera case over his shoulder.

Morgan followed, stopping long enough to grab the tripod.

It took longer than Morgan expected to reach the observation room on the forty-second floor. Outside the Greenbrier suite, they caught the elevator to the thirty-second floor, then waited for the second elevator that would take them to the forty-second floor. The three circled the observation room, checking out the three hundred sixty-degree view of the city. Jerry motioned to Morgan to set up the tripod in front of the northwest-facing windows while he pulled the long lens from the case and screwed it on the camera.

Naomi shook her head. "I don't think you're going to see anything. Visibility is only about thirty miles––I'm guessing we're close to eighty miles away from Port Clinton."

"I know it's a long-shot, but you never know what may show up in a photo. We might be able to see a plume of black smoke from this distance."

Morgan felt the vibration of her pager. She looked at the screen. "It's the station again. Maybe they have news." She could have kicked herself for leaving the bag phone in the truck. This was probably one of the few times she actually could have gotten a signal. But being at the top of the Terminal Tower had not been on their agenda. "Where's the closest phone?"

Naomi motioned toward the center of the room. "There's a payphone next to the elevator."

"Great. Let's go," Morgan and Naomi turned to leave.

"Hold up. I'm done here." Jerry unscrewed the lens from the camera and put it in its protective bag. "Just give me a minute to pack the camera. Morgan can you give me a hand?"

Morgan walked over and lifted the tripod off the floor, then the three of them headed toward the elevator.

Morgan hadn't thought they could see anything anywhere close to the Lake Erie islands, but at least she had the satisfaction of knowing they were doing something. Half of the tiny town of Marblehead and Kellys Island were inhabited by Tanners––and a handful of them called Port Clinton home. Fearing the worst was causing Morgan gut-wrenching pain. Maybe this call from Sam was news from the Davis-Besse plant or the evacuations.

After setting their gear on the floor, Jerry reached into his pocket and pulled out a handful of change. He handed Morgan a quarter for the call. Her hand shook as she dropped the coin into the slot. The station manager answered immediately.

"Morgan, where are you? This just came in over the National news wire. Palisades Nuclear Plant in Michigan and Nine Mile Point in New York both have had explosions. This story's big—it's National."

"We're on the observation deck of the Terminal Tower. Jerry thought we could see something from here. Even though it's a clear, sunny day, we're too far away."

"Jerry's got a good nose for news. Hey, while you're there have Jerry take a look toward the Perry plant—just a hunch."

Morgan placed her free hand over the mouthpiece and turned to Jerry. "Sam says to see if anything's happening at Perry."

Jerry grabbed his camera case and ran back to the observation windows giving him the best view toward the Eastern shoreline. A minute or two of intense silence went by.

"All looks quiet," he shouted back at Morgan.

"Hey, Sam. Jerry doesn't see anything out by Perry."

"Interesting. Explosions go off at nuclear power plants along the Great Lakes but nothing at Perry? At least nothing yet—mmm, I've got that feeling. Tell Jerry to pack up and get back here."

Right boss, anything you say, boss. Jerry's got the nose for news and I'm just the pretty face with a microphone. She pushed her thoughts to the back of her mind and motioned for Jerry to pack-up. "Okay, Sam, we're heading back."

"What'd he say?" asked Jerry.

"He's got that feeling. The one he gets before a big story pops," Morgan said as she picked up the tripod.

Jerry reached for his gear and glanced back in the direction of Davis-Besse. "Nothing we can do here. Let's get back down to the truck. At least there we have a mobile phone if Sam calls back."

After completing the two separate elevator rides down from the observation deck, Morgan, Jerry, and Naomi stood in the beautifully ornate lobby on the main level. Morgan shook Naomi's hand. "I want to thank you again for meeting us on a Sunday."

"What about the radiation? The evacuations? Should I be worried about my family?" Naomi placed her hand over her heart. "I have a sister in Columbus. Maybe we should go down there until this blows over. What do you think I should do?"

For the first time, Morgan took a studied look at the woman who'd been at her side for the last two hours. Funny how she'd been there yet not. Naomi's petite frame wore the black suit with a narrow black necktie as casually as her skin. The straight skirt fell just below her knees. Her dark-brown, shoulder-length bob framed a rather plain face devoid of makeup. The overall look was of a woman around fifty-ish, in control of her environment, yet unobtrusive. At the moment, though, she was looking to Morgan for direction.

"Naomi, you know as much as I do about what's going on. I'm sure the National Guard will get everything under control quickly. It doesn't seem like Cleveland is in any danger. Why don't you go home, turn on the TV, and watch the local news? Maybe tune in to one of the radio news stations?"

"I guess you're right," Naomi wrung her hands. Her eyes searched Morgan's as if looking for an answer she liked better than going home and turning on the news. A deep furrow etched her brow. "Can you find your way back down to the parking garage?"

"Yes. Jerry and I covered the opening of *The Avenue* last year. Having so many retail shops and restaurants here in this wonderful old building should bring shopping back to the city. I sometimes ride the train down here on a Saturday afternoon––very convenient."

Morgan's pager went off again. "We're on our way, Sam!" she said through clenched teeth before tilting the small black box so she could read the number. "Not Sam. It's my brother, Michael. I'll call him back when we get to the truck."

Morgan picked up Jerry's tripod and turned toward the elevator to the parking garage. She hadn't taken more than a few steps when her pager vibrated once again. She juggled everything so she could see the number. That was odd. Michael rarely called using their special code for an emergency. His emergency couldn't be anywhere near the magnitude of her emergency, and what was going on with the rest of the Tanners living near Davis-Besse. More than the explosion at the nuclear power plant was her concern over the status of her family. Once she and Jerry got back to the station, she could use the phone in her cubicle to make calls to Marblehead. Aunt Mavis, the owner of the local diner, knew everyone within three counties––she would be her first call. Michael's sporting goods store in Painesville, Ohio was closed on Sundays. He always spent the day re-stocking. She'd fill him in on what was happening and he could start making calls. What could possibly be more important than radiation spilling out of Besse?

"I need to call my brother. It should only take a minute and then Jerry and I are out of here."

Naomi pointed to a bank of phones in the lobby's corner nearest the doors facing Public Square.

Morgan hustled across the marble floor and dropped everything at her feet. Jerry was right behind her fishing in his pocket for change. She took the coins and jammed two dimes and a nickel into the slot then punched in her brother's number. He immediately picked up.

"Hello? Michael, I'm in the middle of an emergency situation. There's been an explosion at the Davis-Besse power plant. I don't have any details. I'll call you back in a few minutes from the mobile phone in the truck."

"Listen to me, Morgan. I'm in an emergency too. There are military jeeps with mounted machine guns coming out of the salt mine, for God's sake. One of them just blew up a speedboat not a hundred yards from me! The poor bastard was just trying to get the hell out of here––and––kaboom!"

Morgan rubbed the back of her neck. It was sticky with hair spray. Surely, she'd missed something. Was he talking about a movie he'd seen? He was always giving her a blow by blow of the latest action movies. His heavy breathing brought her thoughts back to what he'd said. "Salt mine? Where are you? What's happening?"

"The Grand River. I came down to work on my boat. I don't know what the hell is going on."

Morgan's stomach tightened. She felt her blood draining away. Jerry had rejoined Naomi at the entrance to the train station. Morgan motioned for them to stay where they were.

Morgan's legs quickly turned to jelly. She leaned against the wall of the Terminal Tower's ornate lobby for support. "Are you sure about this? What do you see now?" A loud sound drowned out her words. "Michael! What was that?"

There was nothing on the line but static. "Michael? Michael?"

"I'm okay. Felt like some kind of explosion. It shook the boat. Whatever––it's close."

Morgan rubbed her forehead. Their Marblehead family was fighting for their lives from Besse's radiation and now Michael's life was in danger. She needed to do something––but what?

"Michael. You need to get to safety."

"Gotta go," he said. Then the line went dead.

"Michael? Michael? What's happening? Don't hang up on me!" Morgan's raised voice brought Jerry and Naomi racing back to her with questioning looks.

Morgan replaced the receiver with the softest of clicks. She sifted through what she knew from the call, separating the facts from her emotions. She could repeat everything to Jerry, as bizarre as it was, but what about Naomi? She was a civilian whom they'd met that morning. She'd been handling the news of the nuclear power plant explosions calmly and offering help when needed. But this was nearly in their back yard––and military jeeps? Jerry and Naomi had reached her side. Oh, what the hell––their world had just crumbled.

"What's up? You look about to collapse. Your brother in some kind of trouble?" Jerry asked while setting the camera bags on the floor.

Morgan straightened, hoping to give the illusion of being in control. She wasn't. Not even close. At the moment it appeared she was the only Tanner that hadn't been thrown into a life or death situation. She gave Jerry and Naomi what little she'd been told including hearing the explosion that was large enough to rock Michael's boat.

"The salt mine? What's the military doing in the salt mine? How can that be? I thought it never shuts down," asked Naomi raising her hands in consternation.

"They shut down for the entire month to install new state of the art equipment. I did a story on it back in January. It's amazing down there. You could easily hide . . ." Jeeps? Yes, there was plenty of room to park a number of vehicles beyond the large doors before taking one of the elevators down into the bowels of the mine.

"Morgan? Hey, Morgan. You remember something else? What the hell's going on?"

Morgan watched as everything Jerry was feeling was etched on his face––incredulous, bewildered, helpless, and most of all fear. But somewhere in all that his nose for news surfaced and took control. He swallowed hard. Gulped. "Better call the station about this!"

"Is this some kind of retaliation attack because we bombed Baghdad?" Naomi asked raising her voice. Panic oozed from her eyes. "What's next? Are there going to be planes dropping bombs on us? The attack on Baghdad was just last January seventeenth. I remember because it was my husband's birthday."

Morgan had been a reporter for the *Washington Post* when the Gulf War, code name Operation Desert Shield, began. She'd been covering the troop buildup and defense of Saudi Arabia against Iraq's invasion. The coalition of forces led by the United States was the daily top news story and Morgan loved the challenge of covering a war––a war over oil. Her articles caught the eye of a network bigwig and here she was now, in Cleveland, Ohio, covering the activities of the local garden clubs.

Desert Storm was still on people's minds. Three months after the final bombings wasn't long enough to erase the kind of horror that had invaded everyone's living room on the nightly news.

Morgan glanced around the large lobby, making sure there was no one close. "You need to keep your voice down. We don't want to create a panic." She turned back to the telephone and slipped another quarter into the slot, then dialed the private number for the station manager. She, too, remembered January seventeenth––like it was yesterday.

Sam picked up on the second ring.

"It's Morgan. We're still at the Terminal Tower. This is going to sound crazy, but there are military jeeps blowing up boats on the Grand River. They're coming out of the salt mine!" Morgan paused a beat. "Tell me you know about this."

"Christ, what the hell is going on today? Yeah. I know about it. We're flooded with calls from Grand River and Fairport Harbor. But how do *you* know about it?"

"My brother just called and told me. He's right there at the sailing club across the river. And Sam, there was one hell of an explosion while we were talking."

"Explosion? I don't know about any explosion. Did he tell you about a caravan of jeeps heading toward Perry?"

"No. Michael could only see them going in an easterly direction. Jerry and I will head back now."

"No. I want you to stay put and find out what the hell's going on out there."

"Look, Sam. We have the satellite truck. We can be in Grand River in a half hour."

"I've already sent Richards and his crew." He paused as if speaking to a child, enunciating each word. "I told you to stay put."

Morgan inhaled through clenched teeth, keeping her frustration under control. "Okay. I'll try calling Michael back, but he's using his bag phone and the reception is sketchy."

Morgan replaced the receiver. She raised her hand before either Naomi or Jerry could ask for the details. She took another quarter from Jerry's outstretched hand and dialed her brother's mobile number. He answered on the first ring.

"Michael, I just talked to Sam. He's getting calls from the neighborhoods in Grand River and Fairport Harbor about the jeeps. They're heading in the direction of the Perry plant. You'd better get out of there . . . now!"

"No can do, Sis. There's a sentry on the river. Whoever these goons are they don't want anyone leaving. That explosion you heard sounded like it was near the mouth of the river. There's only one thing out there––the Coast Guard Station."

"The Coast Guard Station? I'm sure you're wrong."

"Listen, Morgan, I can't hear any sirens. There's no help arriving––period. I have to assume the Coast Guard boats are out of commission."

"What are you going to do?" Morgan was feeling a full-blown panic coming on.

"Stay there and watch. I'll let you know what's happening, but don't call me. I'll call you when it's safe. I don't want to run out of battery power. I'm not so sure about using the ship-to-shore radio. It can make a lot of static noise which might be heard across the river."

Morgan's hand shook. She hung up the phone and turned toward the others. "It looks like there is some type of military attack centered around the Grand River. They may be heading toward the Perry Nuclear Power Plant."

Jerry picked up his gear. "We can't stand around in such a public place with just payphones."

Morgan had to be the one to remain calm and take control. There was a major news story out there and Michael was her eyes and ears at the scene. She needed to stay in contact with her brother, not to mention the rest of the Tanners in the Port Clinton area who were escaping from Besse's radiation. And Sam had ordered them to stay put for further orders. What would she have done back in her days at the *Post* when faced with a sizzling hot story across multiple locations? Lock herself in a room with a dozen phones! "Exactly. Is there an office in the building with multiple phone lines?"

Naomi picked up Jerry's tripod. "Follow me. The security office is down on the lower level. Across from the train station."

Morgan slung her tote bag over her shoulder. "Lead the way."

Naomi motioned with her arm for them to follow. She marched toward the wide staircase and the train tracks below, like a general leading troops into battle.

2

Grand River, 12:00 P.M.

Michael Tanner crouched low in the center of his thirty-six-foot sailboat's main cabin. He couldn't risk any side-to-side movement. Talk about being in the right place at the wrong time. Last fall he'd ended the boating season with the engine spitting and sputtering. But there was no time to do a thorough overhaul––it would have to wait until spring. Friday afternoon, he'd watched as the sleek white hull was gently lifted from her cradle, where she'd spent the long winter months, and taken to the river's edge. Michael's whole being filled with pride as his beloved boat settled herself into the swift moving current of the Grant River. It had taken a bit of finagling to be the first one launched for the season at The Sailing Club. Being a Sunday, his sporting goods store was closed, and he hadn't felt one smidgen of guilt for leaving his family to deal with restocking. After setting the fenders and tying off the dock lines, Michael took a deep breath of cool, refreshing spring air and stepped aboard.

He'd been sprawled over the Cummins diesel with an open-ended wrench in one hand, and a rag in the other when he heard it. The sound, loud enough to break through the music coming from the portable radio sitting on the galley counter, sent chills racing through his body. He'd jerked his head up, cracking it against the floorboards above. Crawling out of the bilge he considered what other vehicles could sound the same as the jeeps he'd driven in the army. With no concern about the rocking motion of the boat, he poked his head out of the hatch. "One, two, three, four camo painted jeeps coming out of the salt mine?" Michael muttered. He scanned the far side of the Grand River. Each jeep had a soldier standing in the back manning a machine gun. "What the hell?" His mind raced for an answer. Maybe the National Guard was doing training maneuvers? Could be. The mine was closed for the month while a new state-of-the-art elevator was installed. It could handle two of the huge tandem axle dump trucks used to haul the salt out of the mine. But surely the whole town would have been buzzing with chatter about Guard maneuvers.

The wake from a speedboat going much too fast sent the sail-boat rocking from side to side. Michael fell sideways, landing on the steps. He braced himself against the bulkhead and peered out the hatch. Three jeeps continued out through the salt mine's gate, heading east. The fourth one stopped, facing the river. The speed-boat slowed, preparing to dock at Pickle Bill's, although the popular seafood restaurant wouldn't be open for a few more hours. Farther upriver a fisherman sat in a small boat, his line floating with the current. A man wearing coveralls and tool belt ran toward the jeep from the adjacent employee parking lot. He began waving his arms and shouting at the soldier. Was this part of the maneuver? Maybe he should grab a cold beer from the cooler he'd brought for the day and climb up on deck to watch the Guard's war games.

The soldier whipped the machine gun around firing at the man. The man flew up off the ground, then dropped in an unnatural pile. At the sound of gunfire, the speedboat made a sudden turn, head-ing back down the river. The soldier turned the gun around, firing at the speedboat. Riddled with bullets, the boat exploded. Through the blazing flames, Michael could just make out the fisherman diving into the river, then swimming toward Ram Island.

A sea of adrenaline rushed through Michael's heart. "Oh, God. These aren't maneuvers. This is real––and I'm a sitting duck."

Michael slowly closed the hatch cover. A sailboat with the hatch open was a boat with someone aboard. He needed to become invisible. Moving back down the few steps, Michael grabbed his mobile phone off the settee. He sat cross-legged on the floor cradling the black case. Willing his heart to slow and his brain to take over in combat mode, he forced his mind back to his days in the Army's Officer Training classes. Understand your enemy. Know your limitations. Formulate a plan.

Who was the enemy? He didn't have a clue. Where had those first three armored jeeps gone? Headed east. What's east? Only a bunch of nurseries . . . and the Perry Nuclear Power Plant.

Michael unzipped the bag and removed the phone's handset. He punched in the number for the Fairport Harbor Police Department. He got a recording saying all circuits were busy, try again. He redialed and waited––still the recording. He leaned back against the settee taking deep, lung-filling breaths. He waited until his heart stopped pounding in his chest. He picked up the phone and tried once more, this time getting a busy signal. He balled his hand, slamming his fist against the cushion. "Hell, I've got Sylvie and the kids to protect," Michael whispered between clenched teeth.

He'd never felt this helpless, not even in his Army days. He needed to get help to his family. There had to be someone he could call to check on them. Warn them. About what? Where the hell were the police––the Coast Guard––the National Guard?

He entered the number where he hoped his wife and sons would be. He let it ring forever. *Come on. Pick up the damn phone!* Sylvie finally answered just as he was about to hang up.

"Hello? I'm sorry we're closed."

"Sylvie, it's me," he whispered. "I'm glad you're at the store."

"You know I am. We agreed over breakfast that the boys and I would unpack the Coleman order. Why are you whispering?"

"I'm on the boat and there's a dangerous situation down here. The boys with you?"

"Yes, of course. Gunner too. Why are you whispering?" she whispered back.

"Listen to me carefully. I want you to follow my directions without question. And don't call me. I can't take any chances one of these goons will hear me talking."

"Goons? What goons? What's going on? Where *are* you? Are you in danger? You need to get out of there. Leave and come to the store."

"Sylvie, you're not listening to me! I *can't* leave!" Michael didn't know how much of what he'd seen to tell her. He didn't want to throw her into any more of a panic than she already was, but she just wasn't getting it. He had to tell her something––maybe not the whole truth––at least not yet.

"Look, Sylvie, there's some kind of local unrest. I guess you could say its gang-related. There was some gunfire and a boat exploded on the river. I'm waiting for the authorities to arrive." He paused long enough to take in a long breath and let it out. "And there's more. I talked to Morgan a few minutes ago. There's been an explosion at the Davis-Besse plant."

"That's impossible. Situations like that don't happen here." Sylvia's voice had risen to a fevered pitch. "A nuclear power plant explosion means radiation. Michael, we live too close to the Perry plant!"

"*Just listen.* Nothing's been said about Perry. I don't want you to upset the boys. Prepare backpacks for each of you and one for Mom. Fit Gunner with one of those new dog backpacks. Fill it with his dry food, water bottles and bowl. Grab one for Saint Nick too. Pack as if you were going on a cold-weather camping trip in the woods. Take enough of the food packages to last several days. Oh, and don't forget a change of clothes for everyone, you won't be able to go home first."

"Michael, you're scaring me!"

"This is serious, Sylvie. Get out of there as quickly as possible and go to my mother's house. And Sylvie––take the Glock."

Sylvia turned on the radio sitting behind the counter and tuned to the all-day national news station. Michael had said an explosion at Davis-Besse. Surely there would be details.

"Breaking news just in. There have been explosions at two additional nuclear power plants. Palisades Nuclear Plant in Michigan and Nine Mile Point in New York both are reporting explosions. We still don't have an update on the current status at the Davis-Besse Nuclear plant in Ohio."

"Oh my, God. This *is* bad." Sylvia said in a panicked voice. She turned up the volume on the radio and hurried around the counter in search of her sons.

She found Nathan and Daniel pulling lanterns and cook-stoves from a large crate. At six and eight, everything was still a game and packing paper was flying in all directions. She didn't want to scare the boys, but they needed to move quickly. "Hey, boys, we're going on an adventure," Sylvia said in her excited mom voice. She then headed over to the display of backpacks. "Help me pack for a short camping trip. Gunner and Saint Nick get one too. Let's see how well you remember what to take. Grandma's coming with us, so pack one for her."

Less than half-an-hour later, they were in the Ford Explorer heading toward her mother-in-law's house on Little Mountain. Sylvia hoped she hadn't forgotten anything in her mad dash through the store, grabbing everything they might need. Might need where? Where were they going? How far? How long? The shelves were now nearly bare of freeze-dried meals, tightly rolled sleeping bags, bug spray, a first aid kit and a case of water. She'd remembered flashlights for everyone and threw in a propane-stove, just in case. She'd probably over packed. Michael always complained about how much gear she took on camping trips. Great Lakes Sporting Goods shop had been in the Tanner family for three generations. It had started out as a small hunting and fishing store in the city of Painesville and doubled in size after World War II. Although the street outside was quiet, Sylvia knew they were too close to the Perry facility to worry about the family business.

She inhaled deeply and focused on the traffic ahead. The Glock wedged between her and the console reminded her just how dangerous this adventure could be. The box of ammunition bulged in her jacket pocket.

3

Little Mountain, 1:00 P.M.

Perched high up on Little Mountain, Katherine Tanner had a bird's-eye view of most of Lake County and the Lake Erie shoreline, which included the Grand River. Little Mountain wasn't actually a mountain, it was a hill, but it was the highest hill in Lake County, and could be seen jutting up from the horizon for as far as the eye could see. Her husband had made a fortune as an executive of Standard Oil. In the mid-fifties, he'd built the modern house cantilevered out over the rocky face of the mountain, like an eagle about to take flight. Now, nearly forty years later, it was also her studio-- the place where magic happened in her paintings and jewelry and pottery. Every day the world changed before those windows, storms came and went, snows blanketed the forests and spring rains filled the waterfalls with wonder. She had always felt safe hidden behind these strong walls, but that all changed with just one phone call from her son. She could see a glow of red peeking out from the plume of black smoke.

The unmistakable thud of the mudroom door slamming against the wall caught her ten-year-old Golden Retriever's attention. Saint Nick headed in the direction of the kitchen, his feet trying desperately to get some traction on the polished oak floor. Katherine followed at a slower pace.

"Grandma, Grandma. Mom says we're going on an adventure!" her grandsons shouted. "And you're coming too!"

Katherine reached the kitchen and held her ground next to the island as the two boys careened into her, nearly knocking her down. Gunner and Saint Nick joined in the fracas until Katherine finally had enough of the out-of-control greeting. "Enough! You all need to settle down or there will be no chocolate chip cookies and milk."

"Okay. Okay," they said in unison, and even the two dogs sat up at the word cookies.

"Help yourselves to the plate on the table, and you know where to find the milk. Your mom and I need to discuss our adventure, so you stay here in the kitchen. Got it?"

"Got it, Grandma. Mom, how many cookies can we have?" asked Nathan.

Sylvia turned to follow her mother-in-law into the living room. "As many as you want," she called over her shoulder. The boys shrugged their shoulders and looked at each other with amazed expressions, then lunged for the plate before their mom changed her mind.

Katherine stood at the wall of glass. "I just got off the phone with Mike before you arrived. He'd already talked to you and said we need to leave the area. He filled me in on what's happening on the river. I think that smoke is the boat that exploded. While he recounted the situation, we heard a helicopter." She pointed to a dark spot moving out over the lake heading toward Perry. "That must be it."

"It doesn't look so bad from here. Michael said it's some sort of local unrest. Maybe that helicopter is the police watching for trouble at the Perry plant. Or maybe the TV 8 news helicopter." Sylvia didn't sound very convincing.

Katherine felt the vibration beneath her feet a second before she heard the explosion.

"Oh my God! What the hell was that? I felt the house shake." Sylvia demanded.

Katherine pointed to a huge billowing cloud of intense black smoke near the shoreline at the mouth of the river. An explosion large enough to shake the house some eight miles away must have contained a large amount of fuel and perhaps vehicles. She studied the location of the dense smoke growing in size, followed by several smaller explosions.

"I think it's the Coast Guard Station," Katherine said as calmly as she could.

"Why aren't we hearing the fire truck's sirens from Fairport Harbor? That speedboat's been burning for awhile now." Sylvia asked, her voice rising.

Katherine wished she had some answers––any answers. The westerly winds pushed the black mushroom across the river. Soon it would envelop the tiny town of Fairport Harbor.

"Mike said there are goons watching him! He can't leave! Maybe that's his boat burning!" Sylvia grabbed her mother-in-law's arm. "Where are the police? Where's our military? Where's the National Guard? Somebody!"

"I don't know." Katherine put her arm around Sylvia's shoulders. Her daughter-in-law was on the verge of hysteria. Understandable. Her husband was in the middle of what amounted to a war zone and she had two small sons to worry about. It quickly became obvious that Katherine would need to keep a level head and get them far away from danger. "Look, Sylvia, we don't know what this is all about, but what I do know is that we need to stay calm and focus. Michael wants us to get somewhere safe."

"So, where's safe?" Sylvia asked. "Maybe Columbus?"

"Look, Mike thinks our military will quickly put a stop to whatever this is. We may be safe up here on Little Mountain from ground attacks, but we're a sitting duck from the air. We need to do what Mike said and find somewhere more remote until our guys can take over."

"I still think we should head south, maybe down around Hocking Hills or somewhere else in mid-Ohio. I want to get as far away from the lake as possible."

Katherine understood Sylvia's thinking. It was her first thought as well. But, whoever they were, they had at least one helicopter in the air. What if they started randomly attacking vehicles on the high-ways? She couldn't risk putting them in that kind of danger.

She stepped away from her daughter-in-law. "Look, why don't you go back to the kitchen and turn on the radio while I pack a few things. Maybe there's some news by now."

It didn't take Katherine more than a couple of minutes to grab a change of clothes and a few toiletries. She stuffed them in a plastic grocery bag and headed to the kitchen.

Sylvia plowed into her as she turned the corner from the hall-way. "The power just went out!" She steadied herself against the wall. "Nothing on the radio."

Whop, whop, whop. They hurried back to the windows. A black helicopter came into view. It didn't have any identifying insignias. Police? Katherine could almost see the pilot. Then a large explosion sent debris high into the air.

The house vibrated and Sylvia screamed.

"We need to get out of here," Sylvia yelled.

If Katherine could see the pilot, then the pilot could see her. He wasn't the police. She grabbed Sylvia's hand. "Come on. We're going to lose ourselves in the most remote areas of the Oakwood Botanical Gardens."

4

Terminal Tower, 1:00 P.M.

Morgan took a few steps inside the security office. The dirty hospital-green walls only added a blanket of gloom to Morgan's mounting anxiety. The smell was reminiscent somewhere between her parents' basement and her high school locker room. She hadn't wanted to hang around either one for very long. And she certainly didn't want to be here now––she wanted to be out helping her family. Jerry edged his way past her and set his camera cases on the floor in the far corner. Then he stood stretching his back.

Naomi closed the door. "I hope this office will work for you. I know it's not the Ritz, but you've got three phone lines and three desks. And you have easy access to the parking garage when your station manager wants you to leave."

Morgan moved to the nearest green, metal desk. It looked as old as the building. She rearranged the scattered papers into a pile and set a greasy clipboard on top, then pushed them aside. The surface appeared clean enough, so she pulled a legal pad and pen from her tote bag. "Thank you, Naomi, this will work." The old wooden desk chair rolled back on rusty wheels, scraping the green linoleum floor. "I'll start making calls to give folks these numbers to use." Morgan eased into the chair. "Jerry, you call the newsroom." Morgan leaned back. The seat rocked ominously from side to side. The swivel chair could use some oil. It could use a new cushion too. Hell . . . just trash the chair.

"Hey, Morgan. I've got the newsroom on three. It's Sam," Jerry said.

Morgan picked up the receiver and pressed the blinking button. "It's me, Sam."

"Listen, Morgan. There's been a second explosion at the Davis-Besse plant. Palisades and Nine Mile Point are reporting second explosions as well."

"How? Wha . . .?"

"Just listen, Morgan. I don't have all the details, but the explosions came from inside the fencing. The Camp Perry National Guard has taken control. As a precaution, they've called for an evacuation of the area."

"Oh my, God! My family's there!" Morgan balled her fists in frustration. She needed to do something. "Jerry and I can be there in a little over an hour."

"I've already got Schneider and Wilson on the way. They took the satellite truck and can transmit live."

"But it's my *family!* I know the area. Jerry and I can get better coverage."

"No, Morgan. You need to stay right where you are. You can't help your family sitting in the truck on the road with hundreds of other people. This is a huge story. Wilson's my top reporter. I need you to keep your head together. Trust me on this. Wait for my instructions."

"Instructions for what? I know I can do more than these fluff jobs you give me because I'm a woman. Wilson wouldn't be caught dead covering the annual luncheon of the garden club or the current gala at the Union Club. Is the Debutant Ball really newsworthy anymore?"

"That's enough, Morgan. I smell a story here. Something is about to happen––I got that feeling. Stay where you are––that's an order!"

"How about Jerry and I head out to Fairport? That's a big story–– maybe bigger."

"Got Levitt and Cooper on it. Stay put, Morgan!"

"Right, Boss. I'm not moving." She slammed the receiver down. "There's been a second explosion at Davis-Besse and the others. Sam's ordered us to stay here! I'm a reporter, not a telephone operator!"

"Don't know what to say." Jerry crossed his arms over his chest and leaned back. "You have phone lines and can make arrangements for your family to come here. I bet the hotel has plenty of rooms. Just my two cents."

Morgan slumped in her chair. "Damn. What's going on? I feel totally helpless down here! Someone must know what's happening––who's behind these explosions?" Morgan's chair wobbled. She grabbed the edge of the desk. Just her luck to have picked the broken chair to sit in. "What's our government doing––where's our National guard––our military?"

Jerry raised his shoulders in a helpless shrug. "Our pay grade doesn't take us into those exalted circles. Not much we can do but wait."

"That's it! Not us, but I know who can," Morgan reached for her tote bag. She pulled out her address book and flipped through the pages. "My cousin, Travis. Travis Tanner. He's got connections in three counties. He'll know what to do."

For five years, Travis and his wife, Olivia Bentley Tanner, have lived on the Virginia plantation she inherited from her grandmother, except for the summer months. Every first of June, they left the oppressive heat and headed north to the old captain's house on the tip of the Marblehead peninsula. Travis was born and raised in Marblehead and he was quick to brag about how the Lake Erie islands had been his playground. Morgan's vibrating pager stopped all further thoughts. She checked the number on the display. Michael.

Morgan pulled the phone closer. She dialed the number for her brother's bag phone. He answered immediately. "Who's this?" He was whispering again.

"Michael, it's me. Jerry and I are holed up in the lower level of the Terminal Tower. Use this number to call me."

"Okay. Listen . . . "

"Are you okay? What's going on there? Why are you whispering?"

"Listen, Morgan. Just listen. Another jeep just emerged from the salt mine across the river and they're shooting at anything that moves. It still appears they're heading east toward the Perry nuclear plant. There was a huge explosion while I was talking to mom. Looks like it might have been the Coast Guard station. It's definitely out of commission––no help coming from that direction. Where the hell is our National Guard? The police? Anybody?"

"I was just going to call Travis. A second explosion was reported from inside the fencing at Besse. The National Guard has taken control of the plant. There's been an evacuation alert for the area. Maybe Travis can help get our family to a safe place."

"He's already on it. Aunt Mavis called him. She said not to worry about them. He's got busses heading to the ferry docks. They'll be able to get folks off the islands. The police are going door-to-door. There will be a 727 waiting at the Port Clinton Airport. Aunt Mavis said the plan is to fly the evacuees somewhere near Columbus."

Morgan wondered if she should suggest the hotel in the Terminal Tower as a possible destination since besides the busses and plane, people could also come by train. The problem with that might be the fact that Cleveland lay between Besse *and* the Perry plant. Not a good idea if both sites had radiation leaks. Best not get involved. Travis was more than capable of handling the logistics of what could be a massive evacuation.

"Thanks for the info. This makes me feel a lot better. Now, I can focus on you. I'll let you know if I hear anything. I'm sure the National Guard is on their way. Stay safe," Morgan said and disconnected.

Jerry waved his arm to get Morgan's attention. "I have Sam on the line. Any help in Fairport may be awhile," he said to Morgan. "It appears the National Guard is swarming all over the nuclear plants that had the explosions. They're in the middle of total evacuations."

Morgan pressed the lit line two-button to join Jerry's conversation with Sam. "Sam?" All she got was a dial tone. "He hung up!"

"Well, at least downtown Cleveland seems okay," Naomi said with a bit of optimism in her voice.

Jerry's forehead crinkled. He cocked his head as if searching his brain for a fleeting thought. He lifted his chin in Naomi's direction. "Except for the two big Sea Rays I saw approaching the East Ninth Street pier."

"Sea Rays?" asked Naomi.

"Boats. Sleek, fast, expensive boats," Jerry answered.

"There shouldn't be any boats there," Naomi answered with a slight shake of her head. "Nothing special is scheduled until the first of May. Maybe the odd fishing boat, but it doesn't sound like anyone would be fishing from the boats you described."

"I know my boats, and those two babies were at least forty feet with a ton of horsepower. You saw them, didn't you, Morgan?"

She tried to remember what she had seen looking to the north or east while on the observation floor. Her focus was toward the west and Besse. She couldn't remember anything except it was a beautiful, clear day. "No, I didn't," she answered. "Sorry."

"I'm telling you, something's up! Those boats don't belong––not in April."

"Jerry, does it really matter? We have a story to cover."

"This is *Cleveland*, not Miami. Toys like that aren't brought out of mothballs until the heat of summer. Then, guys with lean, tanned bodies cruise up and down the Cuyahoga, past diners on colorful patios to ogle the beautiful women in bikinis at their sides." Jerry waved his arm in an irritated gesture. "They don't belong at the East Ninth Street pier in *April!*"

They don't belong. "Huh," Morgan said out loud. They don't belong––they don't belong. She let his words rattle around in her head. She'd been a reporter long before she'd even considered doing a stint on TV, and Jerry didn't get excited over nothing. She smelled a story. Even a little one would give her something to do. Sitting in the basement of the Terminal Tower waiting for instructions wasn't working. She was nothing more than a messenger in a rabbit hole. They had to split up if she were to have eyes on the city.

"Jerry, you need to get back up to the observation deck. Keep an eye on those boats and anything else that looks out of place."

He pushed his chair back, stood, and in two steps was lifting his camera case off the floor then heading toward the door.

"There's an emergency phone box on the south wall of the observation deck, near the elevator. I'll write down these phone numbers for you." Naomi pulled a pad of paper and pencil from the corner of the desk and jotted down the three lines. She then stood and took a few steps over to a rack of keys on the wall near the door. She handed both the paper and several keys to Jerry. "Here's the key for the emergency phone box, the elevator key for the observation floor, and the door. Answer the phone if it rings. I'll have one of the security guards meet you at the elevator and take you up."

The phone on Morgan's desk rang. She pressed the button with the blinking light. "Security office, Morgan speaking." She paused for just a second. "Michael, are you okay?"

"Yeah. Listen. After we hung up things went crazy down here."

"That was just a few minutes ago. What could be more crazy than guys in jeeps shooting at people and boats blowing up?" Morgan asked with what she hoped was a bit of humor.

"Well, it *sounds* worse! I finished talking to you and then heard what I took to be the air horns of half a dozen eighteen-wheelers coming from Fairport. That was followed by car horns. Like the horn of every resident in town, then police sirens and fire trucks––all blaring at the same time . . . Then . . ."

"What the hell is going on?"

"Don't interrupt. It gets worse!" Michael paused to take a breath. "I eased over to the starboard settee and peeked out the window. That's when the explosions began––one right after another. Flames shot in the air from five or six different locations. The car horns and sirens stopped."

"Michael, you need to get out of there!"

"And go where?" Michael sounded exhausted. "I've been sitting here racking my brain thinking there may be a way for me to sneak off the boat and swim underwater to a safe place and walk into town. But now there's a black cloud of smoke hovering over Fairport. Looks like this might be the safest place. If I haven't been shot at yet, then those goons don't see a sailboat as a threat."

This was an unexpected turn in what was already a series of bizarre events. Fairport Harbor? There couldn't be more than two thousand residents. With the Grand River bordering on the west and Lake Erie to the north and the wasteland of the former Diamond Shamrock Alkali plant to the east, why would anyone care about Fairport? Except—that it was a stone's throw from the Perry Nuclear plant.

"You're right. This new development doesn't make any sense. I'll call Sam. I bet his police scanners are lighting up." Morgan was about to hang up when she remembered Jerry's comment about the speedboats docking at the East Ninth Street pier. "Hey, do you know anything about high-end Sea Ray's coming into the city for anything? It's too early in the season for pleasure boats to be on the lake, and from Jerry's description they don't look to be commercial."

"Nope. Can't help you there, Sis. But definitely out of the norm."

"Jerry's heading back up to the observation deck. Maybe he can see what's going on with those boats."

Morgan disconnected. A man in a security uniform entered the room. Naomi handed him Jerry's tripod and battery pack. After he was loaded down with equipment, he headed to the elevator.

Morgan immediately called Sam at the station to fill him in on her brother's calls. Her reporter's instinct told her not to mention the speedboats––at least not until there was a real story––and it would be all hers.

Naomi sat down at the desk next to Morgan's. "That call didn't sound good, trouble with Sam? Michael?"

Morgan tapped her pencil against the desk. It had the rhythmic tat-a-tat beat of a mind searching through the hodge-podge of notes she'd taken during her conversation with Michael. "No. It wasn't good," she answered Naomi.

"Well? Are you going to give me the details?" Naomi asked.

"I have an idea," muttered Morgan.

Morgan flipped over the page and began drawing a map of the Great Lakes and the positions of the three nuclear power plants that had explosions. Just for the heck of it, she added the Perry plant. She didn't see an obvious connection between them except that Cleveland seemed somewhat in the middle. Morgan flipped the page over and began drawing another map, this time of downtown Cleveland. She didn't have a concrete reason for doing so. It was just her reporter's instinct—and she always followed her hunches. She started with Public Square and the Cuyahoga River and went as far as East Ninth. Then she filled in the major landmarks and buildings as close as she could remember.

After a brief knock, a man entered the office wearing the uniform of the maintenance department. "Hey, Miss Naomi, I just saw Mac and that cameraman heading up. Thought you might need some help down here."

"Thanks, Lamar." Naomi turned to face Morgan. "I'd like you to meet, Lamar Hill. He's our best maintenance man."

Morgan reached out her hand and stared into the eyes of the biggest black man she'd ever seen. "Nice to meet you." His hand was as big as a catcher's mitt and as strong as a vise grip. He could have been a linebacker for the Browns.

Naomi motioned toward the chair opposite Morgan's. "Have a seat and we'll fill you in."

Morgan positioned the separate sheets of paper in a row across the desk without acknowledging Naomi's comment. "This is making even less sense," she mumbled.

The phone rang. Naomi answered, then handed it to Morgan. "It's Jerry."

Morgan glanced at the large, round schoolhouse clock on the wall. Jerry and Mac had left twenty minutes ago. She hoped he had something. "What've you got?"

"Mac got us to a higher, off-limits floor so we had a good view of the pier. Four men got off each boat. They off-loaded some kind of motorized carts onto the dock. A bunch of what looked like canvas tarps were taken off the boats and stacked on the carts. Like some kind of flatbed hauler with a guy operating it from a platform at the rear. They headed up Ninth then turned west on Lakeside. They passed City Hall and turned down East Sixth Street. I lost them somewhere around the auditorium."

Morgan drew a square building, labeling it City Hall, then another for the auditorium on the page containing the city map. In the margin, she scribbled the word tarps. What the hell? Motorized carts? Why would anyone move stacks of tarps on something as large as motorized transporters down city streets? And why bring them in on expensive speedboats? Why not trucks––or one eighteen-wheeler? There had to be more to it. And they didn't just vanish.

"Morgan, they're gone now! So are the boats. Two of the guys stayed behind after getting the transporters loaded and on their way. They got back onboard and took off.

"Hmm. Which direction did they go?"

"East. They headed east––fast"

"Thanks, Jerry. Stay there and keep watching. Maybe check the Cuyahoga River. This is crazy."

Morgan heard the door open behind her then two people entered wearing white uniforms similar to those worn by kitchen staff. They set a large platter of sandwiches down on a side table along with a plate of cookies. There was also a tub filled with ice and soft drinks.

"I thought we all could use something to eat. I called over to the hotel's chef while you were on the phone," Naomi said while removing lids and arranging a stack of paper plates and napkins.

"I'm starving!" Lamar said and jumped up from his chair.

Naomi moved to Morgan's side. "Your last call sounded weird. So now what do we do? Should I call the police and have them check it out?"

The reporter part of Morgan's brain kicked into high gear. Adrenalin rushed through her veins. "I need to get to the Auditorium. But how do I get there without them seeing me? It's Sunday. The city has to be like a ghost town. There's no way to just blend in with a crowd."

Naomi and Lamar, with a sandwich in his hand, looked at each other and said in unison. "The tunnels!"

5

Michael Tanner crawled along the floor toward the head––he had to pee. The Catalina's bathroom was located near the bow––just a few more feet. He'd have to stand and move slowly into the portside facility. Any sudden move from side to side could be disastrous––the swaying motion would give away that there was an occupant on board. The bigger the boat the less rocking––he hoped thirty-six feet was big enough. He didn't want a hull full of lead.

After completing that task, Michael crawled back to the center of the cabin, rested his back against the settee and stretched out his legs. He had no more than gotten settled when the ringing bag phone echoed throughout the cabin. Reaching up, he pulled the leather case onto his lap. "Hello?" he whispered.

"Honey, it's me."

"Sylvie, where are you?" The reception wasn't good and he could only catch every couple of words. "Oakwood? Gorge? Yeah, you should be safe there, tons of places to hide. Did you get everything you'll need? I'm not sure how long this is going to last, not even sure what it's all about." He listened patiently to his wife's concerns, then interrupted. "Listen, Sylvie, we have to conserve battery power. I can't start the generator to recharge and there's no power for you anywhere near the gorge. I'll keep in touch with Morgan and the station."

"I'm scared," Sylvia's voice cracked.

"Listen. We're going to get through this. You have to believe that. Take care of Mom and the boys. Sylvie––" He paused thinking of all the things he wanted to say to her. About all the times he hadn't bothered to tell her how much he appreciated her, what a wonderful wife and mother she was. "I love you."

He felt like he was letting her down, he was her husband and she depended on him. But this was bigger than anything he had ever encountered and he needed to keep his wits about him. Sylvie was strong-willed and could take care of herself and the boys, but this would put her to a new test. She would need to keep a level head and she sometimes had a difficult time doing that where their sons were concerned. Navigating the gorge could be tough even for the seasoned hiker and camping would have its own challenges. But the boys had been camping long before they could walk, and his mother was a pro when it came to the outdoors. The problem was she was getting up in years and it had been a long time since she had set a tent stake.

"Sylvie, I'm going to lose power. Be careful. I love you."

The bag phone's battery died seconds after disconnecting with his wife. Any contact with the world beyond the boat's hull also died. Starting the generator wasn't an option. He could just hear the reverberations of the sound along the river, then the machine gun fire–– then death. No, he needed to find another power source. He raked both hands through his hair then laced his fingers together, resting them on top of his head. *Think.* What had he done when he first arrived after unlocking the hatch cover and opening the boat to the morning's cool air? Michael searched his brain for the answer.

Seconds went by. "Right," he murmured. Anticipating that he might need power, he'd plugged the long yellow cord into the dockside electrical box, then wrapped a section around a cleat so it wouldn't fall into the water. He'd heard a crash below and glass breaking. Rushing down the cabin ladder, he saw that the bottle of beer he'd opened and set on the counter had fallen over and rolled onto the floor. It took awhile to clean up the broken glass and wipe down the floor. He'd forgotten all about connecting the electrical cord to the outlet on the outside of the boat.

Michael eased up onto the starboard settee and peeked out the window. There it was, just as he'd left it. But how to get it plugged in when he couldn't leave the cabin? At least not through the aft hatch he'd closed what seemed like eons ago. If the stern faced the jeep, what about the bow hatch? It was already open. He could crawl out and get to the power cord. *Yes.* He waved his arms in celebration of the plan. Then dropped them in defeat. How to do that without being seen from the opposite shore?

After several minutes of debating the possible success and certain failures of several plans he came up with an unrealistic one that just might work. The biggest obstacle would be blending into the very whiteness of the boat. He needed to lose the jeans and navy sweat-shirt with the billowing sail and sailing club logo on the front. He needed to be white. A search of the locker in the forward cabin pro-duced some clothes left over from last summer. He changed into white pants and the plain white t-shirt he used to sleep in, then wrapped his dark hair in one of Sylvie's white silk scarves. He was now ready to go topside.

Standing on the forward berth, Michael pulled himself up through the open hatch and did a belly flop on the deck. The world around him was now clearly visible. Black smoke enveloped the entire mouth of the Grand River––the location of the Coast Guard Station. To the east, more thick black smoke hovered over Fairport, the acrid air heavy. Michael braced his shoe against the edge of the hatch and pushed as hard as he could to reach the starboard rail. He grabbed the closest stanchion and pulled while pushing off with his foot. His rubber sole squeaked as it came in contact with the slick deck. The sound screamed in Michael's ears. He held his breath waiting for the onslaught of bullets. He waited a full minute before kicking the offending shoes down the hatch to the berth below.

Checking to make sure the height of the cabin would shield him from any dangerous eyes across the river, Michael pulled himself along the starboard deck toward the electrical outlet near the stern. Not happy with his slow progress along the narrow space, he grabbed the next stanchion with his left hand and dug in his toes. He focused all his energy in one massive push and pull.

Ouch!! He'd landed with the pointed end of a stainless steel cleat in his belly. It knocked the wind out of him. He melted in a pool of pain. Michael buried his cheek against the cool deck and waited. Waited for any sign that he'd been found out. Had he called out in pain? He couldn't remember. He listened for any movement on the opposite bank––nothing––nothing but the sound of the river slapping against the hull. The fire in his gut began to ease. Michael checked the front of his shirt––no blood. He turned his head to gauge how much further until he reached the plug––another eight feet, maybe ten. He closed his eyes, praying to God to give him the strength to continue.

He reached the power cord before he needed to shimmy over another cleat. After inserting the plug into the outlet and twisting to lock, he leaned against the cabin to catch his breath. He glanced back toward the bow. The return trip along the deck didn't appear quite so daunting and he'd find a way to ease himself over that damn instrument of torture.

It could be a long wait before the battery for his bag phone would be charged enough to use. The highly polished teak floor was hard. Michael slowly pulled the cushion from the bench on the starboard side onto the floor. One of Sylvie's decorative pillows came along with it––the one with the life preserver stitched on the front. Perhaps it would save his butt from getting too sore. The afternoon sun beat down on the cabin roof, heating the interior. Michael leaned over and pulled a cold beer from the cooler. He popped the cap and placed the wet bottle against his throbbing stomach. He'd be paying for this a while. It hurt just to breathe. He settled back to wait for Travis's call.

It seemed like forever since Michael had talked to Sylvie and still the guard sat alone watching the river. If all of the vehicles had left the salt mine, then what was this guy waiting for? He had already damaged the boats that were capable of leaving and any poor soul still in the area was laying low. He felt safe, as safe as one could feel under the circumstances. A sailboat surely would appear as no threat––at least it hadn't so far.

6

Oakwood Botanical Gardens, 1:45 P.M.

Katherine closed the door of the black Ford Explorer behind her, then ran over to the gate and punched in the numbers for the combination lock. The maple syrup events were over for the year and the woodshed of Oakwood Botanical Gardens' sugar shack would be empty. It only took a minute for the long metal gate to swing open. She watched the SUV drive through and closed the gate behind it, listening for it to click and lock.

Katherine got back in the vehicle and pulled the door shut. She didn't bother with her seat belt. "Drive to the end of the lane. There should be just enough room in the woodshed to hide this thing. Then we'll head for the gorge."

Sylvia slid the shifter into DRIVE and focused on the dirt road ahead. "Why couldn't we have parked closer to the gorge? I thought it was on the farm's property. This seems a long way to hike with the boys."

"Grandfather kept the most isolated and dangerous areas on the farm's hundred acres, so it would be rough going in anything but a truck or ATV. The sugar shack is off the beaten path and protected. I don't know what those guys in that helicopter are aiming at, but so far things are blowing up and there's nothing out here but thousands of acres. Besides, as a Board member, I have access to everything. We have options."

"And just how does that help us? We're still too close to the Perry plant." Sylvia asked in a frightened voice.

Sylvia was right, they were close––about thirty miles from Perry. And far too close to whatever was happening in Fairport. But she didn't want to be hours away from her son. No, she would find a way to keep her family safe. They had over three thousand acres in which to hide. She would make that happen––or die trying.

"We can disappear!" Katherine said in a raised voice. She looked behind to make sure her words hadn't upset the boys. They hadn't, but she'd need to be careful not to let her anxiety show.

Katherine glanced at her left wrist. Mickey Mouse's big, gloved hands waved. She should have grabbed the rugged diver's watch from her dresser, but somehow the Christmas gift from her grandsons gave her hope that life would get back to normal soon. It had taken longer than she expected to slide the brown tarp over the SUV as it sat under the protection of the woodshed. It probably wasn't necessary, but Katherine didn't want to take the chance that the sun's reflection off chrome would cause suspicion from the helicopter pilot who had made a sweep of the property just minutes after they'd squeezed the large vehicle into the small space. She watched as her two grandsons ran ahead with backpacks flopping from side to side and Gunner and Saint Nick leading the way.

They were getting close to the gorge and for the first time since that day when her son had brought home a puppy for his sons, she was glad that he had chosen a wolf/husky mix. Sixty percent wolf was enough to scare off any unwanted creatures that might cross their path. She was feeling the weight of her backpack along with the boy's jackets they'd peeled off about a mile back and tossed to her for safekeeping. They'd heard the approach of the helicopter earlier and had huddled under the cover of a stand of pine trees. She didn't want to think what might happen if they were seen out in the open field.

Visions of the news broadcasts of the bombing of Baghdad were still too recent. This wasn't a war they were dealing with, but nonetheless, there were plenty of explosions. She needed to keep her family safe and prayed that Michael wouldn't do anything stupid or heroic.

The boys suddenly stopped and with the enthusiasm and energy that only children possess, began jumping up and down with arms waving. "We're here! Can we go down the hill?"

"No! You need to wait for us," Sylvia shouted. The dogs hadn't listened to the command and had kept on going and were soon out of sight.

The well-marked trail down through the trees was easily negotiated. The leaves wouldn't appear on the tall maple and beech trees for another month so the sun had had a chance to dry out the path. But the going got tough along the creek where the spring rains brought the water rushing through, covering the trail in some places. The adventurous brothers found alternate routes up and around the many large boulders and through the deep crevasses of the sheer rock walls of the gorge.

Half an hour later they were faced with a waterfall so swollen that the path ahead was now under water. She should have expected this. It happened every spring. There was just no way around the waterfall. "Hey boys, we need to find a way to the other side of the creek." Katherine shouted.

"We passed that fallen tree a few minutes ago," Sylvia said while adjusting her backpack. "We can get across the creek there and continue on around the waterfall."

The tree was more than a few minutes back. Katherine kept the boys at her side while their mother tested the tree. It must have come down in a recent storm. The rough bark was still firmly attached and didn't give under her weight. The dogs bounded across first and Saint Nick stood barking his encouragement for his people to follow.

Katherine watched as each one made it easily across. A few years ago, she could have made it as easily as a gymnast on a balance beam. But she wasn't as steady on her feet now. She took a deep breath and stepped up onto the narrow log then tested the grip of her hiking boots by slowly sliding her foot forward then back. She'd walked many logs in her day, but not for a long time. Her legs had never felt like jelly before or her back so sore. She kept her eyes focused on those waiting on the other end as she placed one foot in front of the other and prayed she wouldn't lose her balance.

"Come on Grandma, you can make it!" the boys shouted.

Katherine breathed a sigh of relief as she jumped down onto solid ground. She bent down, resting her hands on her thighs. She took several deep breaths of the cool, damp air. Her legs screamed with fatigue.

"Hey, Kate do you know a place where we can take a break for lunch? I'm sure the boys are getting hungry."

Katherine felt Sylvia's eyes on her. She sensed her assessing the struggle her mother-in-law was having to keep up and wondering if she was too old to continue. Katherine stood and nodded. Her legs were still a bit shaky. She needed to rest––but she wasn't too old. "Yeah, just ahead a ways, there's a large cave. It will offer shelter and be high enough above the creek to be dry."

The cave turned out to be further than she remembered. It was after three when everyone finished the peanut butter and jelly sandwiches Katherine had made before Sylvia and the boys arrived at the house along with a baggie of her homemade chocolate chip cookies. Without the cumbersome backpacks, the boys were now exploring the carvings on the stone. Some were old, dating more than a hundred years, others just the scratchings of names and recent dates. Hiding in the gorge had sounded like a good idea when Michael first told her they needed to find a place to hide away from populated areas. The last time she'd been to the gorge was probably a good twenty years, and it had been in July. Now with the creek swollen, the rocks were slippery and in many places the trail was impassable. Not to mention that it was at least ten degrees colder in the deep canyon than it had been at the start of their so-called *adventure.*

"You're so quiet. What are you thinking?" Sylvia asked.

The sudden question startled Katherine. There were few sounds in the gorge, just the birds and the ever-present rushing of the water over rocks––and the laughter of her grandsons. Unfortunately, the tranquility was dotted with the occasional explosion, siren, and the whop––whop of the helicopter. Katherine took a deep breath before answering. "We can't stay here. It's too cold and damp. And as the day wears on and the sun moves further to the west, it's only going to get colder."

Sylvia glanced over at the boys. "But whoever is out there, even in the helicopter, won't see us here. I think we're safe. We'll collect wood for a fire. Isn't this the cave that you and your dad used to camp out in? We can spend the night."

"It is, but I was a kid and it was summer. It seemed bigger back then. I can't see us spending the night. Besides, we'll need to keep the fire going and that will draw attention. Damp wood creates a lot of smoke."

"But where can we go?" Sylvia pleaded. "We're in the middle of *nowhere*."

Katherine knew exactly where they were . . . her childhood home. Her great great-grandfather had bought nearly a thousand acres of cheap farmland in Lake County, Ohio. Cheap because much of it was difficult to plow due to large glassier deposits of stone left behind after the Ice Age. Growing up, Katherine's father had loved exploring the vast rocky areas containing medieval-like cliffs and streams with fairy-like flora and fauna. He chose to study horticulture at the Royal Botanic Gardens at Kew in England. His dream was to create beautiful gardens at Oakwood Farm that everyone could enjoy. Katherine inherited a hundred acres on Little Mountain from her grandfather on which her husband would build their house. Her father kept a hundred acres containing the family farmhouse and with the rest of the land created the Oakwood Botanical Gardens.

Katherine had been giving an alternate location a lot of thought. She was cold to the bone and the dampness was torturing her arthritis.

"We can hike back to the car and drive over to the Visitor's Center. It would be warm, and we'd have bathrooms."

"I don't know. We've come so far, and the going hasn't been easy." Sylvia watched her sons trying to catch a toad. "I'm guessing it would take us more than an hour just to get back to the sugar shack." Another explosion caused the boys to run back to their mother. "We'd be in a rather large building and we don't know what they're blowing up or why."

Thoughts of crossing the log again had Katherine searching for another option. "I remember an old hunting and fishing cabin. It's on land that Oakwood acquired a couple of years ago. We let the rangers fix it up to use on their days off."

"How far do you think it is from here?"

"I'm guessing about half an hour. Maybe less," Katherine hoped she was right.

Sylvia kept a watchful eye on her sons now wearing heavy jackets to keep warm. Gunner and Saint Nick stretched out in a patch of sun to guard the opening. "I don't know. I think this cave would be safer. That helicopter worries me."

The explosions continued, along with sirens going in all directions. Theoretically, none of those guys out there would consider this remote location as a good place to bomb. But Katherine also had enough camping experience to know that a cave in April would be a cold and uncomfortable place to bed-down––not to mention what wild animals might be calling it home. She had to think about the safety of her grandsons.

Sylvia turned to face Katherine. "Do you know how to get to the cabin from here?"

7

Lamar pulled a keycard from his breast pocket and inserted it into the slot of a rather new looking lock on the heavy steel door leading into the tunnels that snaked under the streets of Cleveland. He stood to the side and gave a sweeping gesture for Morgan to enter.

Morgan hesitated for just a moment. She quickly squelched an uneasy premonition. This was, after all, just a shortcut to her big story. "I feel like Alice about to enter the rabbit hole."

Lamar followed and pulled the door closed behind him. "Pretty much the same thing. Hope you're not squeamish."

Dim lights glowed with a ghoulish haze of grime. "I'm a reporter. I've seen worse."

Lamar chuckled. "Just watch where you step."

Morgan kept close behind Lamar. She pulled the front of her jacket up over her nose. The stench would take some getting used to. Urine, oil, dirt, rust and feces came to mind. But what kind of feces she wasn't sure. She gave herself a mental slap. Growing up a Tanner meant growing up tough with more male cousins than female. Snakes, rats, and other vermin were just something you lived with on Kellys Island. How different could this be from exploring the caves of Put-in-Bay?

Morgan was still thinking about her childhood and watching her feet and what she may be walking through when Lamar came to a sudden stop. She hadn't noticed him reach his right arm back in a protective gesture. She walked right into him.

"Hey dude, what are you doin' down here?"

Morgan steadied herself against Lamar's back. Out of the corner of her eye she saw a mouse, or maybe a rat, run across her path. She stepped to the side to see a short, rather disheveled, man with a dark complexion and long black hair that fell from a center part.

"You bringin' your lady friend down here for a tour of the city?"

Morgan dropped the front of her jacket in an attempt to show she didn't mind the stench.

"I thought you two were moving on. You know you can't stay down here," said Lamar in an authoritative voice.

"Dude, give us a break. We're still in our winter digs. Another month and we'll be movin' on to fresher air." He took a few steps closer and looked Morgan up and down. "Aren't you gonna introduce us to this pretty *white* lady?"

Morgan didn't want to be introduced, and she certainly didn't want to be referred to in a racial kind of way. This white lady wanted to move on and was already having second thoughts about this shortcut to the Auditorium when Lamar stepped aside. "Morgan Tanner, this is Miguel and over there holding up the wall is his buddy, Stan."

Stan gave a polite nod in Morgan's direction then turned his attention to Lamar. "I don't mean to sound like I own the place or anything, but why is a giant of a man like you, bringing a rather pretty lady down here where you don't belong?"

"Yeah, man! This ain't right!" Miguel's attention went from Lamar to Morgan. "You okay, lady? I'll take him out if he's messin' with ya."

It appeared to Morgan that it could have been weeks since Miguel had felt the cleansing spray of a shower or a change of clean clothes. She stepped back as the combination of body odor and filth assaulted her sense of smell.

"I know you haven't heard what's going on out there." Lamar raised his chin toward the ceiling. "But I need to get Morgan over to the Auditorium."

"Dude, does it look like we hang around watching the tube all day?"

Stan's eyes crinkled at the corners as he took a closer look at Morgan. "That's where I've seen you. You're a TV reporter." He moved out into the center of the tunnel. "So, what's happening that's important enough for you to enter this hell hole?" He took a long look at her attire from neck to shoes. "There are nice clean streets above that will take you to the Auditorium. And you won't be ruining those pretty shoes."

Morgan looked into eyes as gray as the tunnel walls. "It started with an explosion at the Davis-Besse Nuclear Power Plant, then there was one at Palisades Point in Michigan, and another at Nine Mile Island in New York." Why was she giving this information to a homeless man? Why would he care? He was slowing her down.

"So, what are you doing in a tunnel under the city of Cleveland? Shouldn't you be with a film crew waiting for something to go down at the Perry plant? Wouldn't that be next? Or are you figuring this is the safest place if there's a meltdown?"

Morgan rolled her eyes. She took one step forward ready to challenge this misfit of society. Her blood simmered just below the boiling point. Her face tingled with the glow of red. She was not some bimbo reporter ready to hide at the first sign of trouble.

Lamar quickly stepped forward, taking Morgan's arm. "Come on we're wasting time. We've got a long way to go and you're not exactly dressed for a hike."

"Hey man, we can help. This is our turf! Where ya goin'?" Miguel asked.

Morgan stopped and turned to face Miguel. "Okay, here's the short version. The town of Grand River is overrun with armed military jeeps coming out of the salt mine and heading in the direction of Perry. They blew up a speedboat, and it looks like they took out the Coast Guard Station. My cameraman saw two high-powered boats dock at the East Ninth Street pier. They off-loaded some kind of motorized material movers then disappeared."

"How are boats docked at the pier connected with explosions at nuclear power plants that are nowhere near Cleveland?" Stan asked, sounding more than a little confused.

"They're not. I obviously can't cover the power plant story and I'm here––*now*," Morgan replied as if she were talking to a child.

"So, what's the story? Two boats docking in Cleveland is newsworthy?" Stan asked with a shrug of his shoulders. "I don't get it."

Morgan seethed with indignation. How dare a homeless man question her professionalism? What gave him the right to challenge her actions? "There may be a story. And if there is––I want to be the first on the scene," Morgan fired back.

"Look, we're on our way to see if we can get closer without being seen," Lamar said as he moved to push Miguel aside.

"Whoa, lady! You're goin' to check out dudes who might have machine guns and all you have to protect you is a man who fixes toilets?"

"A really *big* man." Morgan took a deep breath. This was against her better judgment, but what did she have to lose? And these guys obviously knew the tunnels. "Okay, we can use your help. It looked like six men were heading toward the Public Auditorium."

"Stan, you get 'em close enough for a look-see and find out what game these dudes are playin'. I'll catch up after I get us some toys of our own," Miguel said as he turned to head back, further into the tunnel.

Stan continued to assess the situation that had suddenly turned their quiet Sunday upside-down. He'd made some real progress with Miguel over the last two years. He couldn't let his hard work be undone by a reporter doing a story about the abandoned tunnels under the city of Cleveland. They'd have every nosey adventure-seeking idiot invading their space. Miguel was still emotionally fragile and there was just no telling what he would do. If he went off in another mental meltdown, innocent people could die. He needed to help Morgan get to the Auditorium. Hopefully she'd figure out what was going on with the mystery men and move on. She'd soon realize she wasn't dressed for an underground tour and beg him to get her back into fresh air. He needed to get rid of her before she decided the tunnels would make a story worth telling––tunnels that everyone but a few old-timers had forgotten about.

He couldn't tell the actual color of Morgan's eyes in the murky light. But her outward show of determination didn't hide the uncertainty that looked back at him. He remembered all too clearly what that felt like. "Stay here with Lamar." Stan looked her up and down. "I can move a lot faster than you. I'll check out the area and be right back."

Stan took the shortest route to the Auditorium, not the most direct, Superior to East Sixth. Also, not the most maintained, the storms of last week left sections with inches of standing water. The tunnel ended at a steel ladder. He climbed to the top and exited through a partially rusted door into an alley. He squatted in the doorway of the building across the street. The homeless could sit in plain sight and not be seen by the average passerby.

He waited fifteen minutes without seeing a single person, let alone six men on motorized carts. He surveyed the entire length of East Sixth. Nothing. Not a single soul. Not even Stubby, who on a Sunday could be seen raiding dumpsters.

Stan was fuming when he reentered the tunnel at St. Clair. He'd been sent on a wild goose chase by a TV chick with an overactive imagination. He was done playing games.

Lamar and Miss Tanner were right where he'd left them. Why couldn't she have had enough of the cold, damp, stench and gone back to the warmth of the Terminal Tower? He stood before her waiting for some snide remark that she'd been mistaken. But all he read on that beautiful face was impatience––toward him. Like he'd taken too long.

"There's no one there," Stan said. Short and sweet. Now maybe she'd leave.

"They're up there! I'll just find them myself!" Morgan tried to push him aside.

Stan grabbed her arm. "I'm telling you there's no sign of six men with motorized carts anywhere near the Auditorium."

Morgan gave him a look that clearly said she wasn't about to let this homeless know-it-all stop her. "Lamar, call Naomi and find out what's going on. Jerry must have gotten back down to the office by now. Hopefully, he knows where these guys went."

"Sorry, Morgan. We're out of range for the walkie-talkie. We need a phone."

"Okay, I'll find a phone and call Jerry. Get me up to the street," said Morgan.

Stan let go of her arm. "No. You can't be seen. If I recognized you, they may as well. They'll wonder what a reporter is doing nosing around. That could put you in danger. Lamar, you need to make the call, I'll go up and check again."

Lamar glanced back down the tunnel. "Where the hell is Miguel? He should have been back by now."

Stan was wondering the same thing.

Stan watched Morgan look down at her expensive black suede pumps, now covered in splotches of greasy brown.

"I'll be okay," Morgan said to Lamar. "I promise not to wander off. Just don't decide to go sightseeing. I'm sure Miguel will show up before you get back."

Stan recognized the helpless look in her eyes—yet she maintained control. He liked that.

"One more thing, Lamar. The TV 8 truck is parked in the garage near the door. Bring back my bag phone. It's on the floor of the pas- senger seat."

Lamar shook his head. "You'll never get reception down here. Those big things will just weigh you down."

"Let me worry about that. I would feel better if I had it with me."

Lamar shrugged his shoulders. "Okay, you're the boss."

Morgan watched Lamar and Stan disappear through the steel door that would lead them to the street above. This wasn't going as planned. She stood in the center of the narrow space, afraid to touch anything. The royal-blue wool suit she'd chosen looked great for the camera but would attract grime like a magnet. She didn't want to think about rats or contaminated slime. She wrapped her arms around her waist and focused on getting answers to whether the activity at the pier was somehow tied to what was happening in Grand River. The fact that she'd teamed up with a couple of homeless guys didn't seem important at the moment. With every sound, she glanced back down the dimly lit tunnel hoping to see Miguel's black hair that draped well past his shoulders, and a beard that only slightly hid a pockmarked face.

The incessant drip of water off in the distance was getting on Morgan's nerves. She'd been left alone too long. Something was very wrong. The rusty door finally opened with Lamar rushing through first. "Naomi's in a panic! She can't handle this alone. There's no one with her and Jerry said he lost the guys. They just disappeared! He doesn't know what to do and the station manager is putting pressure on him for answers." Lamar took the bag phone from his shoulder and handed it to Morgan. "Don't know what good this thing is gonna do you."

Stan entered closing the door behind him. "I'm sorry, Miss Tanner, there's nothing out-of-the-ordinary happening out there. And there are no boats at the pier. I guess there's nothing left but to take you back to the security office."

Morgan's heart sank. Her gut said the two events were tied together somehow. Her reporter's instinct was shouting that there was more. She couldn't give up yet.

Stan glanced around. "Where the hell is Miguel?"

Just then the door swung open banging the wall. Miguel entered brushing the hair back from his forehead. "We got a fuckin' problem!"

8

Katherine prayed she was correct on the location of the cabin. They had literally crawled out of the gorge and it had taken its toll on her already aching joints. Following the trail out would have taken them too far in the wrong direction so they had made the decision to make their own way. She had a vague idea of the direction to take and a compass to keep them on course. Gunner seemed to understand the need to take a shorter way out and ran ahead several times, only to come back down. On the fourth try both dogs stayed on top of the high walls of the gorge, barking down on the group below. She was exhausted and didn't know how much further she could go without a break. Even Saint Nick had slowed down.

The helicopter could be heard making another sweep of the area. "Kate, I'm not so sure this was a good idea, they may be able to see us. I'm worried about the boys," said Sylvia.

Katherine watched Nathan and Daniel jumping over fallen trees and pretending they were army scouts searching for the enemy. It was still all a game for them. Then the ground shook with another explosion. The boys stopped and looked back at their mom.

"Stay closer to us, boys," Sylvia shouted. "I'm scared, Kate!"

"We couldn't stay in that cave. The creek is still rushing from the last rain and it's far too damp and slippery. Can you imagine trying to keep the boys warm and dry all night?" Katherine nodded in the direction of the helicopter. "And it's looking like this isn't going to be over anytime soon. We have to find the cabin!"

A short time later Katherine sat down on the log her grand-sons had climbed over a few minutes before. "Let's take a break. I think we can all use a snack. We're safe enough as long as we stay under the cover of these pine trees." But, if her memory was correct, and they actually were in the location she'd calculated, they would eventually have to cross at last one large field to get to the cabin.

"Do you even know where the cabin is, or are you just guessing? Tell me the truth, Kate," Sylvia pleaded.

It was as if Sylvia was reading her mind. "I know which farm it's on."

"Great! Are we close? Are we at least heading in the right direction?" Sylvia's raised voice wasn't loud enough to alarm her sons, who were back to exploring.

"I'm a Board member, not a ranger! Oakwood Botanical Gardens has grown to nearly two thousand acres! I review maps, go on tours, study reports––attend luncheons! I'm tired, too! This is scaring the hell out of me, but do you really want to hear that?" Katherine stood and reached down for her backpack. "Come on, it can't be that much further."

Nathan and Daniel stopped at the end of the tree line. "Stay here and hold onto Gunner's collar," said Nathan. He motioned for Saint Nick to follow and ran back. "Hey, Grandma, the woods stopped! Where do we go next?"

Katherine pulled the compass from her jacket pocket, turning it one way and then another. She wished she were better at reading the darn thing. "I'm not sure. I wish we could get higher so I could see over that rise ahead. The cabin has to be in this area."

Nathan gave a yelp of approval and ran back to his brother. "Grandma says we have to climb a tree to see over that hill!"

"*No!* That isn't what I said!" Katherine shouted.

Both boys were mid-way up the tree by the time mother and grandmother reached them. Nathan wrapped his arms around the trunk and looked down. "See how good we can climb, Grandma?"

Gunner and Saint Nick both stood on their hind legs with front paws resting on the tree, as if their attention would keep the young lads safe.

"You're doing great! You're both talented explorers! Now, what do you see?" Katherine asked.

"Be careful!" Sylvia shouted, while wringing her hands.

Daniel continued to climb. Then he stopped and looked down. "I can't see a cabin. But I still can go higher!"

Nathan clung to the trunk of the tall Maple watching as his older brother reached the top. "Aren't you afraid?" Nathan pleaded with his brother. "How are you going to get down?"

"I'm just older. It's easy," he shouted back. Another couple of branches and he paused. "I see it! I can see the cabin!" He pointed in the direction then climbed back down. "Follow me. I know the way," Daniel exclaimed with great excitement.

"You actually *lock* a place that looks like this?" Sylvia wasn't impressed with the tiny cabin that looked like it hadn't seen a coat of paint in a few decades. Especially since they'd crossed an open field to get there.

Katherine struggled with the lockbox. "Everything gets locked."

The door swung in on noiseless hinges. "Well that's one thing that gets attention." Sylvia felt a little better as she followed Katherine into the single room. With the few windows shuttered, the only light was from the open door. "This doesn't look so bad." She searched the walls on either side of the door. "There's no light switch." She looked up at the ceiling and glanced around the room. "There aren't any light bulbs anywhere or a refrigerator. Kate, there's no electricity!"

"Okay. So, there wasn't any power in the cave either, and you didn't seem to have a problem with that. We're camping!"

"Looks like well-water. There's a hand pump at the sink."

"Wonderful, indoor plumbing!" Katherine set her backpack on the floor. "I'd open the shutters, but we may be here awhile and we can't afford to bring attention to ourselves."

"Mom, can we sleep here on the bunk beds?" Daniel shouted as he climbed the ladder.

Nathan ran past to the second ladder. "Yeah, Mom, this is great!"

Sylvia got a glimpse of dust billowing up as the boys jumped from one set of bunk beds to the other. "Maybe we could open at least one window and see what we're dealing with in here. We can always close it when it gets dark." She hoped it turned out better than it smelled. "It looks like this could be a good place to spend the night. I see a wood stove over in the corner."

"One rule for using the cabin is the rangers leave it as they found it. Doesn't look like anyone bothered to clean."

"Maybe it was dirty when they got here so they didn't see a reason to clean before they left," Sylvia added.

"They come here to have fun. The last were probably snowmobilers." In the dim light, it didn't look all that bad, but she didn't want to take chances with her grandson's safety. "I'll open a shutter. You check the cupboards."

Sylvia tripped on the boy's backpacks as she went in the direction of what looked like a sink. Tossing the bags on the lower bunk she turned back toward the sink as light streamed in through half of the window.

Outside, Katherine twisted the bracket in place securing the second shutter. The sudden vicious barking meant the dogs found something they didn't like. She closed the door to the cabin, so whatever was outside didn't get inside. She found the dogs at the lean-to attached to the side of the cabin. Gunner was on top of the woodpile attempting to pull the top row of logs down while Saint Nick gave encouragement from below.

Katherine glanced around looking for something that could be used as a weapon if need be. There was something behind the stack of wood and all she knew for sure was that Sylvia had the Glock––and she was inside the cabin. Her eyes caught sight of a pry-bar resting against the cabin wall. The cold steel gave her the needed courage to coax the intruder out of its hiding place. She wasn't sure whether she would rather face an angry wild animal that might attack, or a person that could overpower her.

"Whoever you are, I have a weapon." Katherine took the steel rod and hit the closest log a few times hoping it would show whoever was behind the pile that she meant business.

"Gunner, down!" Just then a scrambling Gunner turned with a growl followed by a raccoon that narrowly missed Katherine's leg. Saint Nick was close on its heels while Gunner leaped from the shifting pile of wood. Both dogs were frantically trying to climb the nearest apple tree where the raccoon rested just out of their reach.

"What's wrong?" Sylvia shouted from the door she'd opened just enough to allow her to see the commotion outside, but not enough for the boys to squeeze through. The makeshift weapon in her mother-in-law's hand didn't go unnoticed.

"The dogs found a raccoon. Nothing to worry about."

The boys pulled open the door and ran toward the barking dogs. "This place is the best, Grandma! Can we see the raccoon?" Daniel yelled.

Katherine put her arm around her grandson. "I think this show is over, let's go back to the cabin." She watched as Gunner and Saint Nick did some major sniffing in the area of the apple grove. "Even the dogs have lost interest in this game."

The three were nearly to the cabin when Nathan started hopping from one foot to the other. "Grandma, where's the bathroom?"

"I saw an outhouse in the lean-to, next to the woodpile. The door with the shape of the moon cut out." She took Nathan's hand and headed to the facility. "Let's go see if there's toilet paper."

Sylvia shook her head with a despairing look. "That was my next question."

The two boys ran ahead. "You don't have to come, Grandma. We can find it. We know all about outhouses." Daniel called back over his shoulder.

"Look for a coffee can or something that would protect the paper from critters," Katherine shouted. She glanced back in the direction of the dogs. Gunner was trotting off with his nose held high in the air. He had picked up a scent. She just prayed it was as innocent as the raccoon.

An hour later Katherine whacked off two-thirds of a broom-handle with the ax she'd found resting against the woodpile. She took it and an old rusty hubcap into the cabin. She raised the two items over her head. "Look. Now we have a brush and dustpan!"

Sylvia threw up her arms in desperation. Tears flowed freely down her cheeks. "We can't stay here!" She set the rag on the edge of the sink. "There's mouse shit everywhere! What are we going to do?"

At the first sign that mice, and probably rats, had been the primary residents of the cabin, Katherine propped open the door and used the pry-bar to pull back the remaining shutters. She too wanted to cry but she had to appear in control, even if she was fresh out of answers and with absolutely no other options. Hunkered down in the cold, damp cave, it had seemed the perfect solution. Dry shelter, a wood stove for heat, bunk beds and canned food could hold them safely for days. But that wasn't what awaited them on closer inspection. Someone had left a bag of potato chips in the cupboard and the canned food and utensils were covered in shit as the mice devoured the chips and most of the bag. The thin mattresses that rested on wood planks were nothing more than nests for the breeding of more mice. Within minutes of arriving, Katherine and Sylvia dragged all four mattresses outside.

"Well——" Katherine turned the hubcap one-way and then another. "Now that we have a dustpan, I can sweep off the bunk beds. And, if I chop off half the broom it will be small enough to get inside the cupboards."

"Kate, you're not listening! What are we going to do?"

"Yes, I heard you. I heard *all* of the times you asked me! And no, I don't know what we're going to do, except to use these." She shoved her new tools closer to Sylvia.

"Even if we open the windows and sweep down the walls and floor . . . it stinks!" Sylvia used the neck of her sweater to wipe away the tears. "And, *member of the Board*, I think your first job on returning to the *real* world, is to have a cleaning crew come in here and disinfect the whole building! And leave behind a gallon of bleach!"

Katherine let out a deep sigh. "I know." Her daughter-in-law had always been the rugged, tough-as-nails kind of person. The perfect mate for her adventure-loving son until the boys came along. But she had become over-protective and Katherine knew that it was up to her to find the answer about what to do next.

"We have sleeping bags and if we make sure the floor is swept clean and we wash down the bunks then it will be better than spending the night outside. The wood stove is useable, and we have the pouches of food you brought from the store."

"But it *stinks*. How do we sleep with that?"

"Maybe the smoke from the stove will be strong enough to overpower the stink."

"Very funny! Like I want the boys to choke all night on the smoke," Sylvia didn't see the humor in her mother-in-law's remark.

Katherine had no viable answers that came to mind. She glanced out the open door and saw her grandsons climbing the apple trees surrounding the cabin. It hadn't taken her long to realize that even with the helicopter's presence, the boys were better off playing outside rather than the filth inside the cabin.

Daniel's voice broke the silence and Katherine's troubled thoughts. "Come on Nate, you can make it. Just don't look down, you can see forever up here!" At least the boys were happy and occupied.

Half an hour later Sylvia and Katherine sat on crude wooden benches placed on either side of a fire pit just off the corner of the cabin. Each keeping an ear tuned in for the helicopter.

Sylvia leaned forward with her elbows resting on her knees, twirling a stick back-and-forth. "There's no disinfectant, nothing to scrub with and I found just one bar of Dial. And I don't think that will work. Even if we do get the cabin to a habitable place, think about the mice and God knows what else is calling it home. They obviously don't need keys and will probably join us during the night."

Katherine stretched her legs out in front of her. The boys moved to another tree further away but still within earshot. Nathan was bravely climbing higher. Neither of the women felt the need to continue speaking the obvious but Katherine knew that one of them would have to come up with a solution before dark. There was one bar of soap. Maybe they could melt the soap in a pot of boiling water and scrub the bunks. She had seen a bucket of sand in the lean-to and remembered a story about how pioneer women used sand to scrub floors. Maybe that would work on the cabin floor and between the two remedies, help dispel the odor. They would need to start now in order to finish before dark. As for the night-time invasion by the current residents . . . well that job would have to be left for Gunner and Saint Nick. After taking a deep, encouraging breath, Katherine was ready to tell Sylvia of her new plan.

"Mom! Grandma!" Both boys were running toward them with the dogs on their heels.

Daniel was the first to reach them. "Mom, there's a little lake over there!" He turned and pointed back in the direction of the far trees. "And I saw horses pulling a wagon full of hay into the side of a hill! It was kinda far away, but I saw it! I saw a man too!"

Sylvia's first reaction was alarm at the thought of a strange man being close by. They were, after all, on private Oakwood land. Under the circumstances it was highly unlikely that her sons saw anything more than what was conjured up in the imagination of an eight-year-old. "Okay. That's very nice. I'm glad you're having fun," Sylvia said in a voice that clearly meant they were making the whole thing up.

"No. Really, Mom. Dan isn't lying," Nathan said excitedly. "There really was a big wagon and it just disappeared into the hill! Just like magic! It was so cool!"

"Katherine, do you know exactly where this cabin is located?" Sylvia asked.

"I'm trying to remember. It's a farm––wedged between the land bordering the gorge and a large estate. I think there's a lot of open land––maybe pastures. The cabin was located in the far corner of the property. I do remember a small lake or pond on the map." Katherine looked off in the distance as if willing herself to see beyond the tree line. "As hard as I try, I just can't remember any homes in the immediate vicinity. We should be sitting in the middle of nowhere––nothing but a small lake for fishing, apple groves and open land for hunting." Yet, there was that nagging picture in her head of how Gunner had taken off with his nose in the air. He was on the scent of something and perhaps it *was* more than a raccoon.

9

Morgan and Stan jumped to the side, giving Miguel room. The steel door slammed shut. "The dudes are in the fuckin' tunnel," Miguel shouted.

"That's impossible!" Stan barked. "I searched the area around the Auditorium."

"And did you find 'em? No. You came up empty!" Miguel pulled up his shirt and reached around his back. He brought out a semi-automatic handgun. "I was in the toy box when I heard voices. I grabbed this and some ammo and headed out."

Morgan watched wide-eyed. "You took that gun from a *toy box?*"

Stan moved away from the door, closer to Morgan. "A few years ago, Miguel found an old storage room in the tunnel. He's been collecting weapons. He calls them his toys. Ever since, the room's been called the toy box."

"I knew this day was coming. I'm ready to defend my country," shouted Miguel.

All color drained from Morgan's face. "Is all this really necessary? There are a few guys with a couple of motorized carts and I agree that it's odd that they know about the tunnels. And even more odd that they want to be down here. But do we need these kinds of weapons?"

Miguel jabbed his index finger at Morgan. "Look lady, I nearly got myself killed defending my country in Nam, and nobody fuckin' cared! But I still love the United States of America. I'm not gonna hide while some mother-fuc . . ."

Stan held up a hand. "Okay! Morgan deals in facts and that's what we need to get right now."

Morgan stepped back to a comfortable distance. "I need to get to a phone." Her heart raced, but she needed to remain in control with a cool head. "Miguel, can you find out exactly where in the tunnel these guys are without shooting them?"

Stan placed himself between Morgan and Miguel. "Lamar, you go with Miguel and determine just where these guys are. Then get word to Naomi in the security office. I'll take Morgan topside to a phone. We won't do anything until we hear from you."

Morgan dared Stan to make a comment on her shoes. His grim look and clenched teeth said all too clearly what he thought about her choice in footwear. Why couldn't she have been wearing anything else but heels? "There's a public phone in the next block but it's going to be rough going. Are you sure you don't want to return to the security office?"

"I'm tougher than I look and I've dealt with a lot worse than a smelly tunnel. Time is wasting," said Morgan with impatience.

"Okay, just remember I gave you an option."

Morgan followed close behind Stan. There wasn't room to walk side-by-side, at least not without touching the walls or bumping into one of the pipes that hung at shoulder level. They rounded a corner into a different tunnel and had gone the length of a city block or so when Morgan noticed what looked like a pile of rubble in the distance. "Are you sure this is the right way? It looks like a dead end ahead."

Stan didn't slow his pace. "One of the newer high-rise office towers was built on the site. They broke through when digging for the foundation and underground parking garage."

He made a sharp turn to the right and down another tunnel that she hadn't noticed was ahead. Actually, Morgan didn't notice much of anything except what she was walking through, like the few puddles she'd jumped and a couple dead rats she'd skirted.

"Be careful ahead."

Stan's words, along with what sounded like a bouncing board, registered through her brain cluttered with maintaining her footing when she stopped suddenly––the floor was gone.

"Whoa!" Morgan put the brakes on and looked up as Stan cleared a narrow wooden board without even slowing down. Then she looked down into a massive hole littered with pieces of what must have been the concrete floor. "What the hell is this? You said it would be rough going––not dangerous!"

"There was a water-main break in the area about a month ago and caused this cave-in. We seldom use this tunnel, so Miguel and I made this temporary fix." He stepped back a foot or two. "It's wider than it looks. You'll be fine. Put one foot in front of the other and focus on the wood in front of your foot and . . . don't look down."

"Isn't there another way? I could slip in these shoes."

"Then take them off. You'll have better control in bare feet."

Morgan considered all she'd walked through. No telling what toxic substances lurked on the surface––she was *not* taking off her shoes.

"Suck it up, Miss Tanner. You're wasting valuable time. I've seen first-timers jump out of planes in less time than you're taking. Tell me you can't make it across eight inches of solid wood. I knew you'd wimp-out along the way. Even a kid wouldn't hesitate. You need to keep to the fluff stories. You're pretty good covering the garden club events."

Morgan seethed with anger toward this audacious, infuriating, penniless know-it-all. How dare he talk to her in that manner? Gritting her teeth and snorting fiery expletives she hefted her tote bag and phone onto her shoulders and eased across the plank as easily as a gymnast on a balance beam.

Stan began clapping as both her feet hit solid ground. "I knew you could do it. It just took a little prodding. You were so mad at me that you never even looked down."

Morgan glanced back at the gaping hole. It must have been a sudden dose of adrenaline that drove her across without a thought for her safety––only thoughts of beating Stan to a pulp.

"Don't worry the others are covered with steel plates," said Stan as he turned and headed down the tunnel.

"Others? The city should be maintaining these better. Someone could get hurt."

Stan glanced over his shoulder. "The city doesn't own them. They were built in 1894 by the company that produces the steam. Except for repair problems with the pipes, we're the only ones down here–– or should be."

After what Morgan estimated to be two or three more blocks the tunnel doubled in width and was in better condition as they came to a steep ramp leading up to double steel doors. Stan pulled a keycard out of his inside jacket pocket and slid it across the lock pad. There was no beep. He tried it again––nothing. "That's funny. It's as if it's been deactivated."

"How did you get a keycard? Shouldn't only authorized personnel have those?"

"I happened to be hanging around when the boxes were installed. The street people can be rather invisible to the average person."

"You *stole* it?" Morgan didn't want to think of him as a thief but it probably went with the lifestyle.

"The stack of cards was sitting in plain sight. I'm sure he never missed them?"

"*Them?* Just how many did you take?"

"Two. Miguel has one too." Stan pulled the lever and stepped back as the door swung in.

They exited the tunnel through wide double doors. Stan explained that they'd been installed in 1921 when construction of the Public Auditorium was well underway. It provided a new means of getting upgraded equipment into the tunnels, hence the ramp leading down. At the time the massive multi-purpose performing arts, entertainment, sports, and exposition facility was the largest of its kind. Eventually, after later renovations and additions, the entrance into the tunnels was forgotten.

Morgan followed Stan to a bench in the plaza near the Auditorium. She wished she hadn't removed her jacket and tossed it on the seat while Jerry was unloading his gear from the van that morning. He'd parked in the underground garage and being a Sunday morning, he'd gotten a spot next to the door. Her jacket was just one more thing she wouldn't have to lug around. Now, her wool suit did little to protect her from the mid-forties temperature. She sat down first, then scooted to the side as much as the bench would allow. Morgan was thankful when Stan eased himself down at the other end, giving her some space between them. Her day was going from bad to worse. There were two homeless men living under the city, and one of them was building an arsenal. Her thoughts drifted from tunnels and guns to the man sitting at her side. The afternoon sun reflected off shoulder-length, sandy-blonde hair that looked amazingly clean compared to Miguel's. His beard, although long, had recently been trimmed. Both set off eyes that were now more blue than gray. He'd left his well-worn jacket open. It looked warm, although a couple of sizes too big. His blue plaid shirt was missing the second button from the top––the collar frayed. He didn't appear to be your average street-person, not that she had any experience with the homeless. Perhaps those living on the streets could be the subject of a future story.

"I can see Miguel as a person living in the tunnels, but not you." Morgan noted his jeans were dirty but not ragged. They hugged his long legs too well to have come out of a dumpster. "Your whole demeanor and vocabulary screams of a higher education. Is this really the way you want to live?"

Stan's eyes darted around the empty plaza. His actions reminded her of the time she'd gone through a week of FBI training for a story she was doing. It seemed a lifetime ago.

Morgan reached in her tote bag and pulled out a sandwich that she'd wrapped in a couple of napkins before she and Lamar headed for the tunnels. She placed the napkins on her lap and tore the crois-sant in two. She handed Stan half.

"Ham salad. My grandmother made the best ham salad sand-wiches. You hardly ever see it anymore." Morgan took a bite. "Mmmm. This is good. Wish I'd grabbed two."

"Thanks," Stan finished it in three bites.

Morgan noticed straight, white teeth between full lips. Nice teeth were one more thing that didn't quite add up about this guy who lived on the streets.

Stan carefully folded up his napkin and shoved it in his pocket. "Miguel wasn't always like this. He was part of my company, a guy that took orders without a flinch. We were both from Cleveland so there was this natural bond between us." Stan leaned forword resting his elbows on his knees, his hands clasped. "He was close to the end of his tour-of-duty when we got ambushed. They came out of nowhere, but Miguel snapped into action and took-out most of the Kong singlehandedly. When his gun jammed, he grabbed the one at his feet, still in the hands of his buddy, lying in a pool of blood. Miguel kept on firing."

Morgan felt a spasm, her blood chilled. "I can't imagine the horror."

"When it was over, Miguel helped carry the wounded to a des-ignated helicopter site. His own wounds were enough to send him stateside and earned him a Purple Heart. He saved my life that day. He always put the lives of others above his own."

"What about his family?"

"He has a brother somewhere. Miguel was very proud of his little brother and wrote often to him and his family. Miguel may have been a little too graphic about his wounds. His brother took off to Canada when it looked like his number might come up. We didn't mention his brother's name after that."

Morgan couldn't imagine dealing with life's tragedies without the support of her family. And now, her family––*all* of her family were in danger––either from radiation or gunfire. "What about his parents?"

Stan glanced around the plaza again. He seemed uneasy but continued. "His wounds took months to heal and by then Miguel was pretty messed up in the head. He just couldn't handle the real world."

Morgan was beginning to understand Miguel, but Stan was still a different story. "What about you? How did you come back into civilian life? Was it hard for you as well?"

"I didn't get out until the end of the war. I contacted Miguel's parents, who live in Tremont. They hadn't seen him in a year. They had no idea where he was but felt he was still in the city. Probably living on the streets."

"How did you find him?"

"It took six months. We'd spent two years together in hell. Talking about growing up in Tremont seemed to make it a little easier for him. His stories about the old streetcar lines, the trains and the bridges over the Cuyahoga River were his best memories. I simply followed the tracks."

"What about you? What were you doing during this time?"

Stan stood. "I had a life to come home to."

The ringing of Morgan's mobile phone ended any further personal conversation. She pulled the handset free of its holder. "Hello?" Morgan paused just long enough to identify the caller. "Naomi, what have you heard?"

"Jerry's reporting that nothing's going on that he can see—except folks are leaving the city. No one here has heard from Michael in an hour or so. Maybe . . . Sam . . . Morgan . . .?" The call broke off.

"I lost the call." Morgan set the receiver down.

"I've been watching traffic heading north on Ninth toward the freeway." Stan moved closer to Morgan. "The radio stations must be carrying the news. Looks like people are leaving the city."

"Yeah. That's what Jerry is seeing. I need to call the station." Morgan punched in Sam's private number.

Stan motioned for Morgan to move to a bench in a more protected area while she waited for the call to go through.

"Hello, can you hear me okay?" she waited for a reply then continued. "Hello, Sam, can you hear me?" Morgan stood and walked back to the spot where she'd received the call from Naomi. After several tries with no success, she walked back to the bench where Stan was waiting. "I can't get a signal. I'll have to use a payphone."

Stan watched Morgan set the mobile phone case on the bench, then rest her tote bag on her knees. She reached in the bag, searching for some unknown item on the bottom. She rolled her eyes, glancing first at the sky, then the ground and everything in-between. Scrunching her face apparently helped her hand locate the desired object. She brought out a small cosmetic bag, followed by a hairbrush, a small can of hair spray, a pocket-size package of tissues, a legal pad and an Instamatic camera. She let out a soft sigh of relief when her fingers found what sounded like a fair number of coins. What the hell was she doing? What could be so important that it took valuable time away from calling the station?

"May I ask what you're searching for?"

Morgan pulled out a napkin like the napkin-wrapped sandwich. "Here," she handed it to Stan. "Cookies. Put them in your pocket for later." She reached back in and pulled her hand out with a triumphant holler. Then she grimaced. "Damn! Nothing but a lot of pennies and two nickels. I thought for sure there would be quarters. I'm always tossing change in there."

Morgan thrust her hand back in the bag.

"With everything you've pulled out already, I would assume there should be a wallet of some kind lurking in the depths."

"I left it in the truck. I didn't see a need for it at the time. I left a pair of sneakers and a jacket there too. Could have used those as well."

Stan reached into his pocket. "Why didn't you just ask me for change?"

Morgan looked up at him with an expression that said he had to be the dumbest man on earth. "Right! Like I'm going to ask a homeless man for money!"

Stan reached into his pocket and handed her a quarter. "You'd be surprised what you find on the ground––if you take the time to look." He opened the front of his coat wider. "I'd offer you my jacket, but I know you wouldn't wear it, no matter how cold you are."

Morgan grabbed the coin. "Thanks," she glared back at him for his snide remark, then ran to the payphone.

By the time Morgan got back to the bench Stan had everything put back in her tote bag. And he'd packed up the bag phone and zipped the leather case.

"I didn't expect you to clean up my mess," Morgan said with a frown.

"Don't worry. I didn't steal anything if that's what you're worried about."

"Stan, I'm sorry. I didn't mean that crack about you being homeless––really."

"Forget it. It's not a problem. Did you learn anything from your call?"

Morgan's chest heaved, followed by a sigh. "I'm not sure how much it helps. Michael called the station a few minutes ago to say there's nothing new going on––still the one guard watching the river. But he's heard a series of explosions close by. Like maybe in Fairport or the old Diamond Shamrock plant. They were big enough to send vibrations through the boat." Morgan shook her head and shrugged in a helpless gesture. "I just don't know. This is way beyond my experience level. I do human-interest stories. I'm no hotshot reporter like Geraldo Rivera that covers a war with bombs falling around him."

"Don't underestimate yourself, you're a great reporter."

"How would you know? Do you even own a TV?"

Stan stood and headed in the direction of the Terminal Tower. He looked back over his shoulder. "Yes, I do . . . Several." It didn't appear she'd heard him.

"Why aren't we going back into the tunnels?" Morgan shouted as she tossed her tote bag over her right shoulder and grabbed her bag phone with her left hand.

Stan slowed to let Morgan catch up. "Because we don't know who those guys are or what they're doing down there. And unlike Miguel, we didn't bring any *toys* with us."

Morgan reached his side. "Oh. Got it," she said in a breathless voice.

She rushed forward with the determination that told him very clearly, she believed she was in charge. He smiled at the warmth rushing through his veins—at the quickening of his heart. He enjoyed watching the way her ass swayed from side to side in her stylish royal blue suit. The white silk blouse beneath was open at the neck. A strand of pearls rested below a beautifully long neck. The pencil-slim skirt ended just below her knees showing off shapely legs. His eyes also didn't miss the brown stains on her black suede pumps or the accompanying splashes on her ankles. In the sunlight her dull brown hair turned to a rich mahogany with strands of gold begging to be caressed. Women like her could get a man in trouble. They had a way of throwing you off-track, forgetting the issues at hand and thinking about dinners in fancy restaurants, real jobs and making love in real beds. His thoughts had ventured off in a dangerous direction and he had to pull himself back to reality. Back to the tunnels and the life of the homeless.

Neither said a word on the hurried walk back to the security office. Stan had his hand on the doorknob when Morgan stopped him. "I'm sorry about what I said back there. That was completely rude of me and totally out-of-character. I don't know how to handle this, and I lashed out."

Stan gave Morgan an encouraging smile. "I know."

Twenty minutes later Morgan followed Lamar and Stan as they re-entered the tunnel but this time, she didn't cover her nose. Either she was getting used to the stench or this new development was far more disturbing. It was hard enough trying to keep up when her low-heeled pumps kept slipping on the slimy floor but going back to the truck to get her sneakers had been out of the question. Especially since she'd forgotten to ask Lamar to bring them back with him when he'd gotten her bag phone. Lamar slowed the pace then stopped at an open doorway and peered inside.

"Hey dude, where ya been? I'd about given up on ya!" Miguel exclaimed.

"Just bringing reinforcements," Lamar said as Stan and Morgan stepped around him and entered the old maintenance room.

"Good to see ya, man. Have you figured out what the fuck's goin' on?"

"Not really." Stan glanced around the room then focused on the corner. "I see you've been messing with your toys."

"Yeah man. Did it while this guy was off gettin' you," Miguel lifted his chin in Lamar's direction. "Didn't want him to learn about our livin' quarters down here. If ya know what I mean?" He gave Lamar and Morgan a quick look. "Guess it don't matter now!"

Morgan did a quick study of the room. Two orange plastic chairs, probably pulled out of some dumpster, sat on either side of a card table with one bent leg. She couldn't imagine where the battered couch came from, much less how they got it down there. It sat against the wall with a plastic egg-crate for an end table. They obviously didn't bother with ashtrays.

Miguel pointed to one of the chairs. She vaguely remembered a similar one in turquoise from her childhood. "Have a seat, lady. Tell us what ya know."

Stan brushed off the chair for Morgan. "It's okay."

Morgan carefully placed her tote bag in her lap and the heavy bag phone on the floor at her feet. She recounted everything she knew from the beginning. "Michael will call Naomi if he sees anything new."

Stan took the other chair. "That still leaves these guys down here. Miguel, what did you see when you searched the tunnels?"

"I didn't see nothin' man! Now let's go after those suckers!"

Stan inhaled deeply and closed his eyes. From what he'd told her while sitting on the bench, Miguel's mind was no longer as sharp as it had been during his military years. Booze and drugs kept him in his own special world. Stan opened his eyes. "Calm down and think! What did you hear?" asked Stan with the voice of authority.

"Some bangin' and swearin'." Miguel thought for a moment. "There was the smell of somethin' burnin', then more swearin'. I ducked back around the corner when I heard guys running."

"What street were you under?"

"Superior——I think," Miguel said while scratching his head as if it would help him remember.

"Were they running toward you or away?" Stan asked in a calm voice.

Miguel cocked his head as if he were trying to hear. "Away——I think." he paused. "Yeah, it was definitely away. And then I heard a door open. It must have been closed for a long time 'cause it made a lot of noise and there was a scrapin' sound."

Morgan focused on Stan's troubled expression. "What's down at that end of the tunnel?" Before he could answer Morgan glanced up at Lamar. "You've got to get back to Naomi and have her find out what buildings are down there!"

Stan moved toward the door. "That's just going to chew up valuable time that we don't have."

Lamar stared at an imaginary spot on the far wall. His eyes scrunched as if it would help dig up a memory. "I think I just might have the answer. In the old days, Ma Bell had a switching closet down here. I think I can patch us into the phone lines if I can find it." He looked over at Miguel. "It would be a small room, just big enough to stand in with lots of wires going into a metal box or panel."

Miguel's eyes lit up. "Shit, yeah man!" He ran to the door. "Follow me."

Lamar didn't say a word but followed Miguel back into the tunnel.

Morgan searched Stan's bearded face. She didn't know what she was looking for. Maybe hope, encouragement, or the assurance that they were going to figure out what this nightmare was all about. Whatever it was, she trusted him. She trusted him to help her find the answers. She pulled the sheets of paper with her drawings of the city out of her tote bag and spread them on the small table. "You live here. Do you have even a guess as to what could be down there that would interest them?"

Stan shifted his chair closer to Morgan's and studied the sheets. "You've done a good job at laying out the events and their locations."

"Except for the three nuclear plant explosions, everything is centered around these two areas. The Grand River and here, with the boats, then the tunnels," Morgan said.

Stan pointed to the areas as they talked. "It started at the salt mine on the river with the military vehicles heading east with explosions along the way."

"They took out the Coast Guard station first, and don't forget the helicopter," added Morgan.

Miguel stormed through the door and headed to what could only be called a pile of junk.

Stan followed him with his eyes. "What are you looking for?"

"The dude needs a phone!" Miguel kept digging. "He thinks it's gonna work." He pulled out a yellow Princess phone. "Found it!"

"We'll be back right away," Miguel said while running back into the tunnel.

Stan's attention went back to the event's timeline. "All the focus was on Lake County going east from the Grand River. It was Jerry's notice of the Sea Rays at the pier that drew your attention. You only came down to the tunnels to find the fastest way to the Auditorium and not to be seen by anyone along the way."

"These guys didn't want to draw attention. After they unloaded the boats, they left and headed west on Lakeside. Jerry lost them near the Auditorium. This still doesn't make sense. What are they planning to do with a pile of tarps?"

"The bigger question is, how did they think they could get motorized transporters into the tunnels?" Stan jammed his index finger on the map. "The double doors in the Auditorium we exited!"

A few minutes later Miguel raced back through the door. He took a moment to catch his breath. "The dude's on the phone. He wants me to tell you those big boats just tied up on the Grand River." He took another deep breath. "Right in front of the jeep with the guard!"

Morgan pulled a pen out of her tote and noted the addition of the boats. She raised her eyes to his. They beamed with excitement, as if they'd just discovered a new planet. "We were right. The two *are* connected!"

That warm feeling washed over him for the second time that day. She'd said *we*. She saw them as a team. His heart filled with the joy of seeing her so excited. "Do you see what this means?" Stan asked.

"Yeah, all eyes had to be on Lake County, assuming the bad guys were hell-bent on getting to the Perry Plant. It would have been the fourth explosion at a nuclear power facility."

"It's all a decoy!" they both said in unison.

Morgan reached for Stan's hand. She grasped his fingers in a tight hold. The warmth of her skin sent a rush of excitement through him. He reached over with his free hand to cover hers.

A soft gasp slipped through her lips. She pulled her hand back as quickly as if she'd touched live wires. "Sorry," she said sheepishly. "I don't know what came over me."

Stan shrugged his shoulders in reply, as if the gesture had meant nothing to him––but it had. He leaned further over the table. "Yeah, it was a decoy––a very expensive and elaborate decoy. But the important question is *why*?" He continued to study the sheets of paper without looking up. "Miguel, have Lamar call Naomi and see if she can get access to the original maps of the tunnels. I want to know what buildings have direct access."

"Yes, Sir." Miguel saluted and took off down the tunnel.

Stan tossed a sheepish grin toward Morgan as if to say, *whatever keeps him on track.*

Morgan leaned back in her chair. "Miguel said he heard pounding and swearing and smelled something burning. I wonder if they're trying to get inside one of the buildings without being seen from the street."

Stan rested his elbows on the table. "It could have been an acetylene torch. That would have produced a burning smell. The original door or access may have been sealed, requiring cutting through. Very few of the buildings have working doors anymore––no need to." Stan steepled his fingers, resting them against his chin. "Whatever it is, it's important enough to create a diversion that's worthy of a military operation."

"Huh." It was faint, but Morgan definitely made the sound. Stan could almost hear her brain working. He caught her staring at him. The slight tilt of her head and tightness around her mouth said that she was mentally picking something apart––he got the feeling it was him. He'd given her far too much information about his personal life while sharing the bench with her. He'd had a major lapse in judgment, something he hadn't done in many years. The last time nearly got him killed––he needed to be careful with this woman who suddenly made him want a real life.

"Got it!" Morgan announced like she'd just won the lottery. "You were Miguel's commanding officer."

Stan didn't answer. She was prying. He guessed that was what reporters did. He'd been so careful these past two years to keep himself and Miguel hidden from the world. He'd made promises, and he wasn't going to let Morgan tear down what he'd worked so hard to create. He needed to get her thinking in another direction.

"What about you? I don't see a wedding ring. How come some guy hasn't snatched you up?"

Morgan didn't answer. He sensed hesitation and unwillingness to talk about her personal life. What could give her such a pained look? She'd been hurt, betrayed. He'd seen that look many times before–– on the faces of servicemen who'd gotten letters from home that broke their hearts.

Morgan stared at a burn mark on the table. Circled it with her finger. "I was engaged a few years ago. We almost made it to the altar, until my fiancé decided at the last minute that he wanted a stay-at-home wife just when my career was about to take off."

"I'm sorry. That had to be devastating."

Morgan shifted in her chair, her eyes focused on the door. "Yeah, well, it's not a problem. I've learned to stay clear of any possible love interests. Guys are impressed at first with the perceived glamour and status of a TV reporter. Then they see the long hours behind a desk doing research for a few minutes on screen."

Morgan's eyes locked with his. "It doesn't take a guy long to figure out that ushering me around town isn't much of a relationship."

Stan felt her pain. The pain of rejection, of humiliation, of having her feelings tossed aside and stomped on.

Neither spoke until Miguel charged through the doorway. "Here's the map of the tunnels. Naomi found one in the file cabinet. But it isn't old." He tossed the rolled document on the table. "She won't be able to get a copy of the original until tomorrow when City Hall opens."

"That's not good enough. We need it *now*. I'll follow you back to the phone. Morgan, stay here and listen for any changes in the tunnel. Shut the door and don't try to leave if you hear anything that sounds like they're coming this way. There's a steel bar you can slide into place when I leave, preventing anyone from getting in."

10

K atherine stood, stretching her aching back. One thing that still pecked away at her thoughts was Gunner's unusual behavior after he went trotting off with his nose in the air. He had been gone long enough to become a concern. Poor old Saint Nick had taken a well-deserved nap in the shade while his buddy went off exploring. It had been ten years ago this month that her husband had passed away suddenly of a heart attack. By December she was still finding her way through life alone. Michael had brought his bride over Christmas Eve to trim the tree, as was the family tradition since Mike was old enough to search the pine forest with his dad for the perfect tree. She'd gone to bed early, feeling alone in the house her husband had created for them. The doorbell jarred her awake at midnight. Thinking that someone had lost their way and was in trouble, she slipped on a chenille robe and slippers and padded to the front door. She flipped on the outside lights. No one was there, so she opened the door to find two beautifully wrapped boxes in shiny gold paper and big red bows. She brought both inside and looked at the tag on the larger one. *TO: Katherine, FROM: Santa.* The larger box was whimpering. She pulled off the top to find a tiny golden bundle of fluff. The puppy pawed and licked her face. The second box contained a collar and leash, bowls, food, and a soft plush bed, but no note. Since it was obviously Santa who'd given her the little guy, she named him Saint Nick. To this day Katherine still didn't know who gave her the companion she so desperately needed.

"What are we going to do, Kate? We can't stay here. I'd rather pitch the tent outside and risk the raccoons than have the boys sleep in this mouse infested cabin!"

"Great, Sylvia! So, go ahead and put up the tent outside! And don't forget to activate the cloaking device so that maniac in the damn helicopter can't see us! Or maybe you'd like us to empty the mountain of firewood in the lean-to and set up in there . . . Oh yeah, then we'll build a wall in front with the hundreds of logs we pull out so that mercenary pilot can't see the tent!" She paused for a breath. "And in case you haven't noticed, that smoke to the north is getting thicker and *blacker*!"

Sylvia hurled the stick she'd been twirling between her fingers as far as she could. "Never mind, Kate. You're right. Coming here was your idea and the boys and I will make the best of it," she shot back sarcastically. "And I *have* noticed that it appears the whole town of Fairport is on fire!"

Katherine knew Sylvia was right, but there were still her ideas about melting the soap and sweeping the floor with sand––although she *had* chopped up the broom. The fact was, she was tired. Too tired to scrub the floor. Too tired to deal with the stink. And she was mentally exhausted. And worse yet, she'd taken it out on Sylvia. They both needed a break from the stress––and each other.

"Look, Sylvia. I'm sorry I snapped at you. This isn't like me. Maybe I just need to step back and clear my head. How about you stay here with the boys and Saint Nick. I'm going to take Gunner and see what's beyond the apple grove and the lake."

"Are you sure that's safe? Maybe we should all go."

"No. I can stay close to the trees and react faster to the helicopter if I'm alone. I don't want to be worrying about you and the boys. Maybe you could set the fire in the stove––get it ready for tonight. I won't be long."

"You don't know what's out there." Sylvia turned toward the cabin. "I'll get the Glock. You need protection."

"No. I'll have enough protection. You keep the gun. I'm taking Gunner."

Katherine's stride slowed. She was about to give up and return to the cabin. There wasn't anything but open fields and trees for as far as she could see. Then Gunner suddenly took off running without making a sound. He'd kept his nose in the air once they passed the edge of the lake and now he darted under a four-board fence. He was certainly on private property––it looked like a pasture. Katherine didn't know whether to follow or wait. The helicopter had made another pass while she was still under the cover of the apple grove. If it followed the same pattern, she should have at least twenty minutes or so before it came back. Her decision was suddenly made when Gunner disappeared around a hill. "What the hell? There isn't a house in sight." Katherine said out loud while crawling between the boards. "Ouch! That hurt." Standing upright, she checked her right palm. A black splinter protruded from the base of her thumb. "Damn!" She scrunched her face and pulled on the bugger––it came out clean–– no blood. "Where the hell did that dog go?" She estimated it wouldn't take more than a of couple minutes to reach the hill if she ran. And the way her luck was running today she'd twist an ankle in a gopher hole! "Gunner!" "Gunner!" She shouted. Then she whistled. "Oh, what the hell," she mumbled into her jacket as she took off at a run.

She was nearly to the hill when the alarm bells went off in her head. Gunner should have come back by now, if nothing more than to make sure she was still following.

"Stop right there!"

The angry male voice stopped Katherine in her tracks. She nearly fell forward. Fear drowned out any concern she had for Gunner's whereabouts. She now looked down the long barrel of a rifle pointed in her direction.

"What the hell are you doing here?" The man shouted in a challenging voice.

Katherine watched in horror as the man and his gun moved closer. Why hadn't she given more thought about what or who she might encounter and taken the Glock? If she didn't return to the cabin, would Sylvia know what to do? Would she keep herself and the boys safe until she could call for help? Katherine needed to stay calm and at least appear in control of the situation. Her eyes slowly followed a well-worn brown leather jacket up to meet intense blue eyes set between deep creases and a rather aristocratic nose. Laugh lines——she wondered about those. And where had he gotten such a golden tan in April?

Katherine pointed to Gunner now trotting back to her side. "I was following my dog." She knew that sounded a little lame out here in the middle of nowhere with explosions off in the distance.

"Looks more like a wolf to me. I saw him snooping around here earlier."

"Ah . . . Mister . . ." Katherine motioned toward the rifle. "Do you think you can point that thing in another direction? I think it's pretty obvious that I'm harmless and it looks like you've already made friends with Gunner."

The gun was lowered to his side. "That still doesn't explain who you are and why you're wandering around on private property when you should be safe at home."

"I guess I sort of lost track of where I was. I didn't realize I'd left Oakwood land." That was a lie. She knew as soon as she crawled through the fence. She just didn't expect to get caught.

"And why are you and *Gunner* out for a walk, in the middle of nowhere, when the world is exploding around us?"

If this man intended to do her harm, he would have done it by now. She needed to show strength. Katherine took a few steps closer and stretched out her arm. "I'm Katherine Tanner. I left my daughter-in-law and her two young sons back at a cabin on the old Stevenson farm."

"That rat-infested place? What were you thinking? That's supposed to be locked so people like you can't get in and hurt themselves!"

Once again, Katherine was reminded that perhaps she had made a bad decision and put her family in danger by leaving them alone. But she didn't need to be lectured by this *farmer*. She wondered how long this idle chitchat was going to continue. "The cabin *was* locked. I have the combination. And unless you have a better suggestion, I need to find a safe place for my family."

"Katherine Tanner of Little Mountain? The artist?" He asked while looking her up and down. He didn't look impressed.

Katherine reached down, placing her hand on Gunner's head. "Yeah." She didn't like the fact that this stranger knew who she was. She didn't recognize him, and apparently he wasn't about to introduce himself.

"I own a couple of your pieces. My wife loved your jewelry designs."

"That's nice. But what are *you* doing out here in the middle of what I assume is your land?" Katherine scanned the area. "And not a house in sight."

"Come on, Katherine Tanner. I want to show you something."

Katherine wondered for just a second or two whether she should follow a stranger who carried a rifle and hadn't given her his name. But what other choice did she have? She tried to place her exact location and remember whose land bordered the Oakwood property and the Stevenson farm. Nothing came to mind. She was too rattled to think straight. It also hadn't escaped her notice that Gunner was trotting off as if he knew where he was going. Then the man with the rifle turned sharply to the right——before dark green double doors.

Sylvia watched her mother-in-law approach the cabin with a stranger. Gunner was already telling Saint Nick that it was time to end his afternoon nap. There appeared to be rather friendly dialogue between the two, although Katherine hadn't mentioned knowing anyone in the immediate area. But they were walking side-by-side in a casual manner, a rifle held at the man's side. Sylvia's hand went to the Glock tucked safely in the large pocket of her jacket.

"Stuart, I'd like you to meet my daughter-in-law, Sylvia Tanner and her sons, Daniel and Nathan. And the Golden Retriever that just brought you a stick to throw is my dog, Saint Nick." Katherine moved to the side to give Sylvia space to join them. "This is Stuart Royal and he's offering us alternative accommodations."

Sylvia glanced from one to the other. "You two know each other?"

"No, although we may have met at a few social occasions. His land borders this."

Sylvia glanced over her shoulder to her sons huddled in the doorway. "Boys, get your stuff together and bring your backpacks out here." Her attention was drawn back to Stuart. "Royal. As in the paint Royals?"

"Yes. I suggest we get this place locked up and move on. We'll keep under the cover of the trees for as long as we can." Stuart scanned the sky. "By my calculations, that helicopter is due to make another sweep."

Another explosion went off. The ground vibrated. It was definitely closer. Sylvia ran to the cabin. "Come on Kate, let's grab our backpacks. We need to get out of here." She'd spent the time while she and the boys were alone to organize the cabin the best she could. The backpacks had never been opened, for fear the contents would take on the stink she just couldn't get rid of, even with the small bottle of liquid soap she'd remembered to pack.

"Wow. Sylvia! You really did a nice job in here," Katherine said while glancing around for anything that might get left behind. "I think it even smells better."

"I found the lantern and a can of kerosene in a cupboard. I grabbed a branch from the pine tree out back and stripped the needles, then smashed them on a plate. Sort of a pine potpourri."

"Great idea, Sylvia."

"Oh, Yeah. I found a *Playboy* magazine shoved in the corner of the top shelf. I used the centerfold for paper to put under the kindling in the stove."

They did a high-five then Katherine headed for the door. "I'll close the shutters while you grab our gear and meet me outside."

A couple of minutes later, Sylvia helped the boys into their backpacks while Katherine locked the door.

"Come on boys," Stuart said while motioning them to follow. "Ready for a new adventure?" Daniel and Nathan followed behind, laughing and shouting as eight and six-year-olds do.

They had just reached a stand of pine trees when the sound of whirling blades got louder. "Sylvia, stand next to that tree trunk and don't move. Boys, stand next to your mom!" Stuart's gaze focused on the distant horizon. "Katherine, stay with me."

Stuart and Katherine each took a collar, keeping the dogs at their sides and waited as another explosion shook the ground.

"Do you think the man in the helicopter will shoot at us?" Katherine whispered.

"You don't need to whisper—–and I really don't know. The funny thing is that I'm sure he saw me crossing the pasture on my first trip with the hay wagon, but nothing happened."

Nathan ran toward Stuart and stopped. "You're the man Dan and I saw when we climbed the tree. You have horses! They were pulling the wagon!"

Stuart put a protective arm around Nathan. "Yep, and that's what's strange. I've moved three wagonloads of hay with the horses without incident. Yet, there have been numerous explosions off in the distance. "Why not shoot at me?"

"What was so important about the hay?" Sylvia asked.

The helicopter was now out of sight. "You'll see later. Right now, we need to move on."

Gunner took the lead with Saint Nick struggling to keep up. Fifteen minutes later everyone arrived at the hill.

"I've seen lots of these old storage sheds built into hillsides, but how is there going to be room enough for all of us if you already have three wagon loads of hay in there?" Sylvia asked as they approached the dark green double doors. "I haven't seen any horses in the pasture we crossed."

Gunner sat patiently at Stuart's feet. They all watched while Stuart pulled back the double doors to reveal another set of doors. The heavy steel doors slid open with little effort.

11

Morgan got up from the chair at the sound of the door opening. Stan glanced around the room. "Why's the door not barred? I told you to drop the steel bar in place when I left."

"The door's not barred because I wanted you to be able to get back in quickly. The bar was heavy," Morgan said putting her hands on her hips. "And what were you doing that you left me alone for hours?" She demanded.

Stan slapped a roll of paper on the table. "You know damn well I wasn't gone all that long––besides I have a copy of the original map of the tunnels."

"How the hell did you accomplish that?" Morgan demanded.

"You just have to know who to ask," Stan said as he unrolled the sheets of paper. "Are you going to help or am I supposed to do this myself?"

Morgan sat down in the opposite chair. Her head churning through possible avenues of how he managed to get the prints on such short notice––and on a Sunday. She came up empty.

"Okay. So according to Miguel, they're not in this tunnel. We're under Euclid Avenue." Stan placed an x over a box on the map. "This square shows the telephone switching room. It's under the Ohio Bell

Telephone Building on Huron Road built in 1927." He used Morgan's pen to follow the tunnels. "We cut over to the Public Auditorium here and went above to the plaza." He placed another x on the map. "They were already gone when we got to the Auditorium. That's on the corner of East Sixth Street and St. Clair." Stan then placed the old and current maps next to each other. "Note that the numbered streets run North and South, and the named streets run East and West."

"Miguel said he was cut off on his return. He had to go up to the street because he heard them on his way to us at East Sixth." Stan compared the two maps. "Means they're in the Superior tunnel." Stan drew a circle around the area on the new map. "These tunnels were the last to be built and are wider so they could easily move equipment down there to make repairs. The oldest sections, closest to Public Square, were already deteriorating by the 1920s. They needed to get new steam pipes and generators installed."

Morgan picked up the old map and held it as close as she could, squinting. "The print is too small. We need a magnifying glass. I don't suppose there's one in that pile over there." She nodded toward the far corner, where Miguel found the Princess phone.

Stan got up and walked over to an old dresser that most likely had spent some time on the side of a road. He opened the top drawer. "Got it!" he handed it to Morgan. "We were looking at stamps the other day."

Morgan shook her head. Somehow, two homeless guys sitting in a dirty hovel under the city looking at stamps didn't surprise her. Twisting the map sideways she read the names. "There's the Public Library, or maybe the US Court House which is down a little further?"

"Right. They're going to go through all this for library books," Stan laughed. "Keep reading."

"The Leader Building and the Federal Reserve Bank."

"Hold on!" Stan reached for the map, but Morgan wouldn't give it up. "The Federal Reserve would be big enough. Maybe they recently took in a huge amount of money or gold."

"No way, Stan. Besides, the vault isn't even in that building."

"How do you know that?"

Morgan tossed the map and the magnifier on the table. "I did a story on its history. It has to be something else. Besides, there's no access to the tunnel."

"Actually, there's no access from any of the old buildings anymore. Some years ago, when the tunnels started deteriorating, all of the basement doors were sealed. Folks that knew about them had been using them as a shortcut from building to building. It became a liability issue."

The door opened with such force that paint chips went flying off the wall. Morgan gasped, grabbing Stan's arm.

Miguel chuckled. "Hey, lady, what's with you? Looks like you were expectin' the bad guys!"

"Knock it off, Miguel. We're all on edge. What have you found out?" Stan stood, then moved over to the door and closed it.

Miguel flopped down on the couch. "I don't like being a fuckin' messenger!"

"What did you find out?" Stan asked in an even tone.

"Nothin'! Nobody knows nothin'! The camera guy's up in the tower looking at nothin'. Naomi's talking on three fuckin' phone lines and knows nothin'!"

His tirade apparently over, Miguel leaned back against the cushion. His face glowed with anger while his foot tapped anxiously on the floor.

Morgan wondered how you calm a man who was ready to explode.

"Okay. Where did you last see these guys?" Stan asked in a calm voice that seemed to have a slightly soothing effect on Miguel.

"Around Superior and Sixth. They were making a lot of noise and I smelled the smoke."

"Are they still there?"

"Yeah, I think. It took me forever to get here 'cause I had to go above ground."

Morgan glanced from Miguel to Stan. "Look, if we're going to assume that it has something to do with the Federal Reserve, then

I need to find out what that something might be. No one is stupid enough to believe they can just break into the Federal Reserve Bank. Besides, the vault isn't even there!"

Stan cocked his head, drawing his eyebrows together. "Well, out with it."

Morgan focused on the table. "I promised not to tell."

"You know something, Morgan." Stan took her hand. "It could be the answer to our situation, or at least send us in the right direction. Talk to me, Morgan. What do you know?"

Morgan's eyes locked on his—pleading. "I gave my word I wouldn't discuss the basement."

"The story you did?"

Morgan nodded.

"Come on, Morgan! Out with it!"

Morgan took a deep breath and let it out slowly. "I did that story on the Federal Reserve about a year ago. It was mostly a historical piece and focused on the magnificent architecture of the building. Jerry and I drove separately. After we finished he left with the equipment and headed back to the station. A new heating and cooling system had recently been installed in the building and was monitored and controlled by computer. They were very proud of the new technology."

Stan shifted from one foot to the other with impatience. "And?"

"We talked about the old steam system that hadn't been used in years and I asked to see it. My tour of the basement was totally off-the-record. There was a maze of corridors leading off in all directions and we finally came to a room with three large vaults. One of the doors was open, showing an empty room. I commented on how large it was and was told that occasionally they have a need to store items on a temporary basis."

Morgan chewed her lower lip before continuing. "We walked over to a large steel door. A series of buttons were pressed on a keypad and a heavy steel bar slid back allowing the door to open. What was behind was the original steam equipment. An octopus of pipes and valves filled the room. But it was the outside wall that drew all the swearing from my guide. Apparently, the whole wall should have been covered with reinforced steel and concrete that couldn't be penetrated. That stopped our tour. He rushed me back up to the lobby so he could make some phone calls. On my drive back to the station I wondered what was behind that wall that needed to be sealed off so well."

Stan smiled and nodded. "Access to the tunnel."

Miguel jumped up from the couch. "Is that what those dudes are doing? Breaking into and emptying the vaults?"

Morgan flinched at the sudden move. Obviously, Stan's calming voice hadn't worked. If she was going to find out what these guys were after, then she needed to get back to the security office. "We don't know what this is all about, but maybe I can find out if you take me back to Naomi. I can make some phone calls from there."

"I'll take Morgan to the security office. Miguel, do you think you can get to the toy box without being seen?"

"Yeah, man."

"Good. Give us some time to get back to the office, then close this place up and get to the toy box. I'll meet you there after I take care of Morgan." Stan rolled up the maps as he talked and slipped them into Morgan's tote bag.

"Do I have to walk the plank again," Morgan asked with more than a little dread.

"Nope. Just a couple steel plates." Stan turned back to Miguel before closing the door behind them. "Get everything ready. We may have to handle this operation ourselves––understand?"

"Understand, Lieutenant."

Morgan hadn't missed the exchange. Miguel still had one foot back in Vietnam, but he'd walk through fire for Stan in the present.

Morgan and Stan entered the security office and saw that Naomi was on the phone. "Here, you'd better handle this. It's your brother." She thrust the receiver in Morgan's direction.

Morgan took the phone from Naomi's outstretched hand. "Hey, Mike. Got something new?" Morgan listened for just a few seconds when she interrupted him. "I'm putting you on speaker. Everyone needs to hear this."

"Hi. A few minutes ago, two vans pulled up near the guard across the river. The doors opened and about a dozen guys got out. They were carrying duffle bags and backpacks that they put in one of the vans. Then it left."

"What about the guys? Did they leave in the van?" Asked Morgan.

"No. The van left without them."

"Was there any lettering on the van? Maybe a logo?"

"No, just a plain white van." Michael paused a beat. "But it looked older and was pretty beat-up."

Morgan tried to digest this new turn. "A dirty, old vehicle could blend in to everyday traffic. I don't suppose you could see the license plate."

"No." Michael gasped. "What the hell?"

There was a lot of static on the line. "Mike, talk to us! What's happening?"

"There are two ambulances coming out of the salt mine. The guys are running toward them."

Morgan shot Stan a puzzled look. "This makes no sense at all. Where are the jeeps?" The call was breaking up. "Mike, I can't hear you," Morgan shouted.

"Let me move closer to the hatch. I might have better reception." The line went dead with just some static. "Can you hear me now? They're getting into the ambulances."

"Yeah, that's better. Are they marked? Any names that you can read?" Stan asked.

"Yeah, one. Tri County Ambulance Service and the other is North Coast Ambulance Service."

"Great, our two largest companies," Morgan said sarcastically. "No one will think twice about seeing them on the roads. I'll call the station and they can contact the necessary agencies."

"No shit!" Michael muttered. "They just pulled away and the guard's gone too. The other white van is still there."

"Okay, Mike. This is your chance to get the hell out of there!"

"I'll give them a few minutes and make sure there's no one left hanging around. God only knows what else could be in that mine."

"Okay, keep safe. I'll call the station." Morgan was just about to hang up when they heard a large explosion. "Mike, are you still there?"

"Yeah, but that one was too close. I felt the boat move."

No one said a thing. It was as if everyone had to catch their breath. Then sirens could be heard in the distance.

Stan moved closer to the phone. "I'm pretty sure the ambulances are heading down here. These guys are getting help with whatever they're up to. We need to find out what that is before they arrive." He glanced to the side at Morgan. She'd gone ashen. "Listen, Mike. Thank you for hanging in there. Your level head and efforts to keep us informed have helped more than you can imagine. Keep your position until you're sure the area is clear. Then proceed to a safe location."

"Yes, Sir." Michael hadn't heard a voice that authoritative since he'd left the army. He felt like saluting. "Whoever you are."

The static became louder, then the call dropped.

"Naomi, get Jerry on the phone. Have him keep an eye on everything around the Federal Reserve Bank building. And get word to us immediately if he sees two ambulances that stop in the area. I'm going to call the station and see if there's anything in the wind about unusual activity with the Feds." Morgan hung up and pushed the phone to the side. "Oh, yeah. Have Jerry watch for a white van that might show up with the ambulances."

"Before you leave, Sam called earlier with wonderful news. He wanted me to tell you there's no radiation. The explosions were loud, and powerful enough to blow out whole sections of fencing. But the buildings and cooling towers were never in danger. I thought you'd like to know that your family is safe."

"Oh my God. This is the best news ever," Morgan squealed. "Thank you." She grabbed Naomi in a fierce hug. "Thank you. Thank you." She turned to Stan with tears streaming down her cheeks. She raised her arms to hug him, then caught herself and stepped back. "Isn't this wonderful? No radiation."

Stan's weak smile didn't reach his eyes. "Yes, it is. That's one less worry for you. But we still have our own problems." He leaned over the desk. "You were going to call your station manager."

Morgan slid her professional face into place and punched in the number for Sam while Stan studied the maps and her notes on the timing of the various events. He was right. She needed to put everything else out of her head and focus. "How long do you think it will take for those ambulances to make it from Grand River?" she asked while waiting for the station manager to pick up. Her eyes locked on the back of Stan's long hair. Why was she asking a homeless man how long it would take the ambulances to get there? He'd probably never set foot in Lake County.

"Depends if they use the sirens and haul ass, or keep it slow and not draw attention. Worst case scenario would be twenty minutes. I'm betting they take their time. Maybe half an hour or so."

Well, so much for not knowing Lake County. For a homeless man, he was full of surprises. Something about him didn't sit right—Morgan just couldn't put her finger on it.

"This whole operation was carried out with military precision. A lot of smoke and mirrors." Stan moved so Morgan could lean in closer. "First, there were the three explosions at the nuclear power plants in three different states which got a lot of National media attention and our National Guard moved in. Then you have what appears to be a foreign military attack on the Perry plant with explosions and a helicopter!"

"But what about us?" Naomi asked.

"Exactly! If it hadn't been for Morgan's story, no one but Miguel and I would have known about the unusual activity in the tunnels. Except for the two boats docking at the pier—which Jerry noticed—everything was happening underground. And who would have believed two bums when we tried to tell the authorities? We would have been locked up for trying to cause a panic."

Morgan circled her arm in a motion that was meant for Sam to speed it up and answer the phone. Of course, he couldn't see that, but it made Morgan feel better to be doing something. "We have to stop those two ambulances before they reach the downtown area. And we can't wait for Sam to get back to us with any news on the Federal Reserve."

"It could take Sam days to get through the mountain of red tape just to be told the Federal Reserve is off-limits," Stan emphasized while pacing back and forth. "We need an inside contact. Someone at the top," he took the phone out of Morgan's hand. "Don't bother with Sam. There isn't time."

Morgan placed both hands on the table. She leaned in. "So, who's at the top?" She threw up her hands in despair. "Like I have a pipeline to the President!"

Stan moved toward the door. "Naomi, you need to stay here and make whatever calls you can to stop those ambulances. Lamar, you're coming with Morgan and me. Do you think you can handle a fight?"

"Four years in Nam with the Army. I only wish we had something like *guns*."

"That's being handled as we speak."

12

Oakwood Botanical Gardens, 5:00 P.M.

Sylvia was nearly knocked down as Nathan and Daniel charged past her and through the doorway before she could tell them to wait. "Wow! Mom look! There's horses in here!"

"Really big black horses. So, we're going to share space with horses," Sylvia said with more than a little sarcasm. "And three wagons stacked with hay." Her nose sent the message to her brain that they were trading the stink of mice and rats in the cabin for the slightly less offensive manure.

"They're Friesians. There are six in here," Stuart said as if it weren't strange at all that they had just walked through a door in the hillside into a stable where horses were being kept.

What troubled Sylvia more than Stuart's casual attitude, was how Katherine didn't look upset or surprised––Sylvia felt as though she'd entered the *Twilight Zone.*

"Okay, so me and the boys will just sit over there on that bale of hay." Sylvia pointed further down the aisle. "At least whoever is flying the helicopter can't see us in here."

Another man stepped out of a stall. "I'll just finish bedding them down, boss. I should be done in about an hour or so."

Any optimism Sylvia felt toward their new digs dropped to the brick floor at the sight of yet another person. Now there were four adults and two children and two dogs to share a stable with six giant horses, and three wagons. The cabin wasn't looking all that bad.

"See you inside, Russ. Come on Sylvia, I have a more comfortable place for you to sit." Stuart motioned for her to follow him around the back of a wagon.

"Mom, can we stay with the horses and help Mr. Russ?"

Sylvia glanced at Russ with a skeptical look. "I'm sure you'll just be in his way." Please say no, she prayed. Leaving her sons with a man she'd met a total of one minute ago wasn't an option.

"Not at all ma'am, I'll put 'em to work."

Stuart and Katherine had already passed through yet another steel door when Sylvia paused to look back over her shoulder. The man, Russ, knelt down on the boys' level. He was asking them if they liked horses. He didn't look like an ax murderer.

"Come on Sylvia, they'll be fine. You're really not going to believe this."

Sylvia followed the excited voice of her mother-in-law. She stopped in total disbelief in the center of a large room that looked more like an outdoor patio overlooking a mountain range. She *had* stepped into the *Twilight Zone*. "We're not in Kansas anymore."

"We're in a bomb shelter," Katherine answered with a laugh.

"I can't believe it." Sylvia looked up at the ceiling that was painted to look like clouds drifting across a clear blue sky. With the turn of a knob, she watched Stuart change the lighting from bright daylight to twilight.

"Back in '59, we were dealing with the Cuban missile crisis. With Cleveland being a major industrial center, my father believed the Soviets could very well send missiles our way. He had the perfect location with this hill, and with an endless supply of money, he could afford to create an imaginary world." Stuart turned up the lighting. "My father hired Chicago designer Marc T. Nielsen to build this to replicate a western resort with small cabins facing this patio. The murals covering the walls were done by a New York artist who did set designs for the theatre."

Stuart pointed to the front of what appeared to be a small cottage. "Three bedrooms and a bath are in there." He turned to the side toward another larger cottage. "This contains the kitchen, laundry and storage areas, also a comfortable living room. It's all supposed to overlook this outdoor activity area complete with tables, chairs for lounging and games."

Katherine walked over to stand on what looked like a shuffle-board court. "I had no idea that shelters could be this elaborate." And it was literally in her backyard.

"Some were even larger, with putting greens, swimming pools, sunken bathtubs and anything else that was possible for the technology of the time. However, most were just single rooms built in suburban backyards."

"It's all amazing, but why provide for horses?" Sylvia asked. She couldn't hear any laughter coming from the other side of the door. If the boys were having fun, she should be able to hear them.

"At the time, *Royalwood Farm* was home to some of this country's most sought after Friesians. In order to keep the bloodlines going he had to protect the top stallions and mares."

"Do you really believe that we could be bombed *now*? That's enough hay out there to feed those horses for a long time," Sylvia asked in a worried tone.

"Let's just say that I gambled on the fact that the helicopter pilot wouldn't think a load of hay was anything to shoot at. That would be a pure waste of ammunition." He motioned for them to sit at a round, wrought iron table with four chairs. "Can I get you ladies some coffee? I have a pot on from earlier in the day. May be a bit strong."

Both Katherine and Sylvia said coffee would be fine and the stronger the better. Stuart returned a minute later with three mugs of steaming caffeine and sat down.

Stuart nodded in the direction of the stable. "There's more out there on those wagons than meets the eye."

Sylvia took a sip then held the mug with both hands. "Where's your family? I only saw the handyman—he called you *boss*."

"My wife, Marjorie, died three years ago." Stuart's face took on a pained expression. "My son is off doing his own thing. It's just me now."

Katherine offered Stuart a comforting smile. "Ah, Marjorie Royal. I knew your wife. She was extremely dedicated to the causes she supported. We worked on several committees together. Her passing was truly a loss to the community."

"I guess I've become somewhat of a recluse. Although we each had our own passions, we were a team that loved our time together. She would have been right at my side today driving one of the wagons, then taking over in here to make it ready for a night's stay or a month. There's still a huge void in my heart." His eyes brimmed with tears. "It would be a truly amazing woman who could ever fill her shoes."

Katherine was enjoying the conversation when she noticed Sylvia's movements of agitation. Her foot tapped, her frown deepened and her eyes continued to dart at the door leading to the stable beyond.

"This is all wonderful. I really appreciate you taking us in, but I'm scared to death. If someone like you is holed up in a bomb shelter, then what chance does my husband have? He's sitting right in the middle of the shooting on the Grand River!" Sylvia set down her mug. "I need to check on my sons."

The whirring fans were the only sound after the door closed behind Sylvia. Several minutes passed before Katherine spoke. "This quiet is rather unnerving after hearing explosions and sirens and calculating the return of the helicopter. I wish there was some way to find out how my son and daughter are doing. At least above ground, we had the occasional cell phone service."

Stuart stood and reached down for Katherine's hand. "Come on. I'll take you to the communication room."

After passing through the living room, Stuart paused at another steel door. He entered a series of numbers on a keypad, and the door slid open with just the slightest sound. Katherine stepped inside the small room. "Wow! This looks like something the CIA designed or maybe NASA."

Stuart laughed. "This is the handiwork of my son and his friends. Growing up, the shelter was a fun place to play. It no longer served its original purpose. But during his college years, he became more interested in the military and the new technology. He would often bring home his friends and work on ideas that, well, to most were just fantasy."

Katherine moved to a long desk lined with computer monitors and several phones. There was also a small television set on another table. There were bundles of electrical wires running up the walls and into the ceiling, like tentacles of some ominous octopus.

"Have a seat and make your calls. I'll be waiting on the patio."

"I promise not to touch anything but the phones."

"Don't worry, everything is shut off. Well, except for the outside cameras."

It was only a few minutes later when Katherine joined Stuart on the faux patio. "Everyone's okay, but they're all too busy to talk right now. They said to stay with you and not take any chances on leaving. I wish we knew what was happening outside. We won't know when the helicopter leaves the area."

The deep frown and sadness in Katherine's eyes said more than her words ever could about how upset she was over the uncertainty of her family. Stuart got up and went back into the communication room and turned on the small TV, then flipped a switch on a panel. "Here, this should make you feel more comfortable."

Katherine watched as the screen lit up with the images of the surrounding countryside. "Wow! There actually *are* cameras outside."

"Feel better?" Stuart gave her a smile. "We'll leave it on so you can take a look anytime you want. Now, let's go see how the kids are doing."

It was difficult for Katherine to relinquish control of their safety to Stuart, even though it felt awfully good to do so. She only knew him by reputation and the few times she'd run into him at local events, he'd been a well-respected gentleman. She decided to put their lives in his hands––at least for now. She followed him to the stable door.

"Hey, Grandma, look at us!" shouted Nathan.

Katherine smiled and waved as she watched her grandsons sitting on the giant horse.

"Mr. Russ is giving us pony rides. Her name is Belladonna." Daniel said as Katherine walked closer.

Sylvia sat on a bale of hay wringing her hands and gasping every time one of her sons made a sudden move. Russ sauntered over to Stuart leaving the horse to continue on her own.

"Don't worry about Bella, she loves kids. She'll feel every muscle twitch and body movement. If you watch closely, you'll see her move her back and shoulders to help them balance. I was just there to lift them up," Russ said to Sylvia as he passed by.

At that moment Bella looked back over her shoulder to check on her riders. Obviously pleased with their ability, she continued slowly down the aisle.

"Well, at least she can't get up any speed in here if she decides to take off," Sylvia said while clutching her hands nervously.

Stuart gave a quick chuckle. "Bella wouldn't take off, even if she were in an open field. Trust me on this––she'll take care of your sons."

Russ stopped next to Stuart. "Renee's still at the house with the kids. The power's still on and they're fine. She's going to fix something for dinner and bring it out after it starts getting dark. She'll use the golf cart and stay along the tree line. I told her about our guests."

Stuart patted him on the back. "Thanks, Russ. I don't know what I would do without you."

Russ nodded at the compliment and went back to Bella's side. Stuart joined Katherine who was leaning up against the wagon closest to the door.

"I take it Renee is Russ's wife and they have children. Are you sure they're safe?" Katherine asked. "Maybe we should bring them out here now."

Stuart's broad smile reached his eyes as he watched Nathan and Daniel laughing on Bella's huge back. He started toward the interior door. "Come on inside. Everyone is doing fine here."

Katherine followed but still worried about Renee and her children. How could they leave her alone to fend for herself with the helicopter and unknown explosions?

"I can read the concern written all over your face. They'll be fine. Renee knows what she's doing. I wouldn't let her stay at the house if I thought she and the kids were in danger."

"I have to say *I'm* worried. Remember, I was out there, and my son is still in real danger. I guess it's just my motherly instincts kicking in."

"Russ has been with me for about fifteen years. He started out as a part-timer during his senior year in high school and continued during two years at Lakeland Community College. He and Renee got married ten years ago. They moved into the bungalow out near the service road gate. Russ manages the estate and Renee takes care of the house and cooks. We're a family and I wouldn't let anything happen to them."

"What about the kids?" Katherine asked, still thinking about her own son.

"Jeremy is six and Emily's four. It's nice having them running around, then they all go home and I'm left with quiet. Kind of like being a grandparent."

Katherine was a grandmother and there was no way she would put the safety of horses over the wellbeing of her grandsons. No way! "But that still doesn't explain why you moved the horses to safety first––and Renee's sons are still out there."

Stuart moved into the living room. He sat down on the couch, patting the cushion next to him. After sitting at a comfortable distance, Katherine turned sideways to face him.

Stuart took a deep breath and let it out slowly. He searched her eyes, as if he were looking for a sign whether he could trust her or not. He didn't see one––but he *wanted* her to know. "I'll tell you." He searched her eyes one more time. "Marjorie talked a lot about you.

She loved the few times she went to your house on Little Mountain. I know the necklace you designed for her meant more than any of the jewelry I bought for her. That piece came from your heart, and she wore it with pride."

"I don't think I'm following this. What does jewelry have to do with moving horses?"

"Your house was personal, a reflection of who you are. She often referred to our house as a museum. Although she was the perfect hostess and could put together elaborate dinner parties with ease, she seldom brought *her* friends home. That's why I know about you, but you don't know me."

"And the horses? Did she like them?"

"As you've probably guessed, I'm the Chairman of the Board of the Royal Paint Company. I have the time to devote to the family's long-standing hobby of breeding Friesians. Fortunately, Marjorie loved them as well and I think some of our happiest times were in the stables."

"So, at the first sign of trouble you moved the horses here."

"There's more to it than horses." He paused to organize his thoughts. "My parents began collecting art on their numerous trips to Europe. Many of the pieces that line the walls of the house will someday be donated to the Cleveland Museum of Art for everyone to enjoy. But for now, they remain with me."

Katherine glanced around the room. "You mean valuable paintings are here too."

"That's a lot of hay out there for half-a-dozen horses. My father considered the safety of his beloved art, as well as his horses, when he built this shelter. Those three wagons are built with reinforced frames of stainless steel that protect millions of dollars-worth in art. The bales of hay are stacked to cover the outside layer of those frames––like skin."

"So, with each wagonload of valuable art, you also brought two valuable horses," Katherine's smile was wide and heartfelt. "Brilliant."

"Don't worry about Renee and the kids. She'll have dinner prepared before she has to turn on any lights in the house. She will leave as soon as she feels it's safe."

Katherine's mind was put to rest about their new accommodations—and Stuart. But as exciting as it all was, she worried about *why* they were there. "How long do you think we'll need to stay here?"

Stuart stood and walked over to the door of the communication room and glanced in the direction of the TV. "I don't know."

13

Morgan stood at the open door and gasped. "You have *got* to be kidding! No way are we going to shoot our way through this!" She waved her arm toward Miguel, whose hair was now pulled tightly back in a ponytail. "He could get us all killed!"

Lamar rushed past Morgan. "Hey, brother, count me in!"

Morgan gave Stan her most pleading look. "He's wearing camouflage fatigues! And where did he get those *boots*?"

"I would think you would be more concerned with the AK-47 slung across his chest," Stan said with a chuckle of amusement.

"This *toy box* is an arsenal!"

"Just settle down little lady. I'll take 'em all out––every one of 'em! No mother fuc . . ."

Stan held up a hand to interrupt Miguel's tirade. "No one is going to do anything without a plan." He turned on a large flashlight sitting on a shelf next to the door. "Miguel, we need more light."

Morgan took in the scene before her. "Can those guys hear us? Maybe we need to close the door."

Miguel lifted the rifle over his head. "No way. They're not even in this tunnel."

"Stan, we still don't know what's going on out there. We just can't start shooting," Morgan warned.

"I know that! But we also know that their activities are centered in the general area of the Federal Reserve." Stan raised a hand before Morgan could make another comment. "We know the money isn't there, but what if it's something else that's stored in the vault for a limited time? They get in through the old tunnel access, get the stuff out, load it onto the motorized carts and leave."

Morgan looked down at the map on the table. She poked her finger on the Grand River. "They get away clean, because everyone is putting out fires in Fairport." She paused to think the operation through. "But how? Take the loot all the way back to the Auditorium where they can drive the carts out of the tunnel? Look, the timing's off. It sounds too risky to me." Morgan pointed to the square representing the Public Auditorium. "But it *is* the perfect pick-up point. The ambulances can pull under cover at the lower entrance by the parking garage, the carts drive out, load the vehicles then speed away with lights flashing, sirens blaring and jump on the freeway around the corner!"

She pulled her hand back and folded her arms across her chest. "And no one will ever know what the bad guys took, because the Feds will never talk."

Stan considered the possibilities. "I agree that scenario would take too long. Once they blow the door, alarms will sound. They have to get out fast. What about the buildings in the same area? Do you remember what they were?"

Morgan thought for a moment. "The new Bank One Building is on the opposite corner, but it's under construction."

"Yeah, no access," Stan added.

"The Leader Building and the old . . . that's it!"

"What's it?"

"The building across the street and next door to the Bank One site is vacant. I bet they're planning to move the carts into the basement and wait until it's safe to leave."

"No. Remember I mentioned that the access doors to all of the old buildings had been sealed. Most of them were welded shut then covered in cement, but a few down in that area, and along East Ninth Street were just welded."

"So it's possible that the door to the basement in that building could have been un-welded. Could be that digging the foundation for Bank One damaged the tunnel and access was needed during construction."

Stan nodded in agreement. "Lamar, I need you to check out the back side or alley of the vacant building across from the Federal Reserve Bank. I know the new Bank One construction site is fenced off but see if there's a loading dock or shipping area."

"Let me go, man. No one looks twice at the homeless."

"No way! At the moment you're looking more like GI Joe the commando!" Morgan argued.

Lamar moved toward the door. "I know which place you're talking about. It won't take me long."

"Come on, Morgan, we're heading up to find the closest phone and see if there's any unusual activity in the area. I think you should call the station and see if anyone has been able to find out what these guys are after."

"Okay," Morgan said while rummaging in her tote bag then pulled out a small book.

"You've got to be kidding me!" Stan laughed. "An address book? How many calls do you want to make?" he asked still laughing.

"Just one. But it's a good one." Morgan waved it in front of Stan.

"What about me?" Miguel asked.

"Wait here and be ready to leave as soon as we all get back. Pick out something for me to use and find a Walther for Morgan. She should be okay with the PPK."

Morgan followed Stan down two tunnels then he stopped at a steel ladder. "I'll go up first and make sure everything looks good," said Stan. Morgan watched him disappear into a small room. After a few seconds, he motioned for her to follow. Morgan found herself in a sort of shed-like enclosure. Stan opened the door and she followed him into the bright sunlight. She squinted while her eyes adjusted.

He took her arm and guided her around a corner and a payphone located next to an enclosed bus stop.

"Why didn't we go to the phone room in the tunnel? It had to have been closer than this?"

"You pulled out a book full of phone numbers. That means to me that you want to make multiple calls to folks you seldom call, and maybe someone whose number you don't want made public."

"Okay, so what?" Morgan gave him a look that he'd suddenly gone dense.

"The Princess phone we jerry-rigged is directly under Ma Bell. I'm sure some machine will pick up that the connection was tapped into––and have the numbers you called on some computer printout."

Morgan glanced around at the empty street. "Oh. Thanks. I didn't think about that."

Twenty minutes later, Morgan and Stan entered the toy box together. Lamar stood before them with an Uzi in his arms. "I'm ready! Oh, yeah, there's a loading dock. The funny thing is, the steel gate's pushed back and the door into the building is unlocked."

Morgan looked up at Stan. "I think we're right. The ambulances will show up there if they're not stopped before."

Stan faced Miguel and Lamar. "Morgan made a call to her cousin Olivia Bentley Tanner. She has connections in DC and may be able to get us some answers as to what is going on. So far the National news is all about the attacks on the nuclear power plants."

"Olivia's on the Board of McLeod and Morrison, the shipbuilder in Norfolk, Virginia. If anyone can rattle some cages on the Hill, it's Olivia," Morgan added.

Miguel placed both hands on his weapon. "Okay. Let's take 'em out!"

"Not so fast, we did find out the National Guard is now at the Perry plant. The old salt mine appears to be quiet and Michael is safe, but he's going to remain on his boat until he's sure he can leave."

Morgan moved to Stan's side. "The problem is the authorities don't know what's going on down here. By the time Michael or Sam clue them in these guys will be long gone . . . as I'm sure was the plan right from the beginning. So, I'm afraid we're on our own."

"Even though there are only four of us and maybe six or eight of them, we still have the advantage of surprise in our favor. We know about them and so far, there's no indication that they have any idea we're here. We also have the advantage of high-powered weapons." Stan held up his hand before Miguel could say anything. "Which we *don't* intend to use unless they fire first."

Morgan imagined a bloodbath with bullets ricocheting off the tunnel walls. "What about all of the additional guys on their way in the ambulances? I have to assume they have weapons in those duffle bags they loaded, once they meet up with the van."

"Exactly. That's why we need to finish this before they arrive," Stan said.

Lamar inched toward Stan. "I pulled the gate to the loading dock back in place and jammed a rod through to hold it secure. It will take them a while to figure out why the gate isn't open and pull the rod free. It won't be much, but it should buy us a little time––and piss 'em off."

Stan patted Lamar's shoulder. "Good job. And there's the chance that if it looks like it's going to take longer to release the gate, the ambulances will move off so as not to draw attention."

Miguel pushed past the others to reach the door. "Come on! We have a mission!"

Morgan glanced down at the small 9mm she held. "It's not very big compared to yours. What good is this going to be?"

Stan chuckled. "It seemed to work just fine for James Bond."

14

Royalwood, 6:00 P.M.

Katherine's attention was drawn to the opening of the stable door. A woman entered letting the door close behind her. She was of medium height, perhaps in her mid-thirties, wearing jeans, and a bulky-knit navy sweater.

"Mr. Royal, can you please give me a hand unloading the golf cart? Russ is busy with the horses and our young guests."

Katherine followed Stuart to her side. "Renee, I'd like you to meet Katherine Tanner. She and Marjorie were friends." Katherine reached out to shake her hand. It was the hand of a woman who wasn't afraid of work—callused and a firm grip. A Cleveland Indians baseball cap covered strawberry-blond hair pulled back in a ponytail.

"Welcome to Royalwood, Mrs. Tanner."

Renee's voice was strong, yet pleasant, articulate and to the point. She didn't hesitate to ask her boss for help. It suddenly hit Katherine—Renee ran Royalwood.

"My friends and family call me Kate."

"Ladies, let's get the cart unloaded." Stuart motioned them through the door.

Katherine was surprised to find the back seat and floor of the cart piled high with every size of container imaginable. Renee and her children must have been squeezed onto the front seat, with the kids sitting on what looked like a forty-pound bag of dog food. Katherine couldn't imagine what it took for her to cook and organize all of this with such short notice—and under the threat of explosions in the distance. Under her petite frame must be an amazingly dynamic woman.

Sylvia stood juggling two foil-covered casseroles and a bag of dinner rolls. "Where to?" she asked.

Renee handed boxes full of groceries to Stuart. "Second sliding door before the living room. You can't miss it." She shouted over her shoulder to Sylvia.

Katherine was the last to enter the kitchen and set the large, heavy dish marked lasagna on the stove. She glanced around the compact room. "Wow, this is a lot of pink. Looks like something right out of a vintage Good Housekeeping magazine."

Stuart set the boxes on the counter. "Pink was my mother's favorite color, but I think this was more the doing of the designer," he said moving toward the door. "I think one more trip will have everything unloaded. I'll just be a minute."

Sylvia appeared mesmerized by the intensity of the room. "You mean they actually made pink appliances?" she asked to no one in particular.

Katherine laughed. "And if pink wasn't to your liking there was also turquoise. Design tastes of the '50s!"

Stuart entered with a stack of containers that went into the refrigerator. "Well that's the last of it. Should hold us for a week at least!"

"No!" Sylvia gasped.

Renee patted Sylvia's arm. "He's kidding."

"She's right. So how about we adjourn to the pretend patio and let Renee do her magic in here." Stuart ushered Sylvia and Katherine through the door just as Nathan and Daniel came running toward them with two other children. Gunner and Saint Nick were at their heels. A black and white Border Collie bounded past and stopped at Stuart's feet as if waiting for directions.

Nathan was the first to grab his mother's hand. "Look Mom. We have new friends and they know all about this place! And Jeremy is six years old too. Same age as me."

Daniel pumped Sylvia's other hand. "Yeah. Jeremy and Emily are fun. We like them a lot."

At four, Emily was the youngest and having a hard time keeping up. She stumbled past everyone and headed into the kitchen.

"Mom, can we show them the toy cabin? We'll be real careful," said Jeremy while little Emily nodded in agreement.

"Later. Wash up now, and take Nathan and Daniel with you. Dinner will be on the table when you get back."

All four children took off for the bathroom with Gunner and Saint Nick at their feet.

Stuart reached down to pat the black and white dog's head. "This is Royal's Lady Elizabeth. We call her Lizzie." She looked up at the sound of her name. "There have always been Border Collies at Royalwood. Marjorie raised and showed her dogs. When travel and the show ring became too strenuous, she used her knowledge of the breed to judge." He gave a hand command that sent Lizzie in the direction of the others.

Russ sauntered over to the group with a wide grin that crinkled the corners of his eyes. "All's good. The kids took an instant liking to each other and after a deal of butt sniffing, so did the dogs." He laughed in Katherine's direction. "Hate to say it ma'am, but I think Saint Nick's in love."

"No worries. He's harmless." Katherine chuckled.

Russ and Stuart added another small table next to the long one on the patio, so everyone had room to sit together. The adults raved over Renee's lasagna, salad with homemade Italian dressing and garlic bread. The kids would have been happier with hotdogs. They were excused from the table long before the cherry and rhubarb pie was brought out. Renee announced there would be warm brownies and ice cream later after the kids were finished playing.

With dinner over, Katherine and Sylvia cleared the table while Renee packaged the leftovers and put them in the fridge. With no dishwasher, Sylvia washed, Katherine dried and Renee put everything away. Their teamwork got the job done in record time.

Renee gave the room her approval with a nod. "Thank you, ladies. I think I'd better check on the men," she left the kitchen and headed toward the stable.

Katherine and Sylvia followed the sound of children's laughter to the toy cabin. They stood in the doorway and stared in disbelief. The walls were lined with shelves piled high with board games and picture puzzles and books . . . lots of books. There was a record player next to a stack of records and small toys. Lined up along one wall were bikes, scooters, pogo sticks and a couple of hula-hoops.

"Chutes and Ladders," Sylvia exclaimed excitedly. "I love Chutes and Ladders. Can I play?" She didn't wait for an answer. She plopped down and sat cross-legged on the floor.

Katherine sensed a presence before she heard Stuart's voice. "Dad didn't want us sitting around doing nothing. There's pretty much everything a child could ask for. And since no one really knew how long one of these shelters would be used, there was also a small schoolroom."

Katherine shook her head in amazement. "The only thing I see missing is a place to ride those bikes. A couple of those look to be adult size."

Stuart grinned. "Want to take an after-dinner walk?"

Katherine wondered how many laps around the pretend patio would constitute a walk, but followed without hesitation.

Only the sound of contented horses munching on hay with the occasional snort was heard as Stuart guided Katherine through the far end of the stable to a set of large wooden doors––big enough to drive a tractor through. He opened it just enough for them to enter and then flipped a switch on the near wall. Katherine gasped at the sight of a room as big as a football field.

"If this shelter was actually needed to sustain life for any period of time, there would have been a need to grow food and provide a place for grazing the horses and of course––bike riding."

Katherine took a few seconds to collect her thoughts. This was more than she could conjure up in her wildest dreams. What kind of mind thought this up? Even more incredible was how was it executed. This would be a perfect story for her daughter's *Secrets of Cleveland* TV show. "But how is this possible?"

"We're under a huge hill. Dad had the money and the connections to literally build an estate underground. Over to your right is an area that would have been fenced in––raised beds would have contained crops. Those pens on your left were for chickens and down further would have been two pastures for the horses."

"But it's all just dirt and no sunlight. How did anything grow?"

Stuart returned to the wall and opened the door to a large metal panel. Suddenly the room was flooded with a blue-tinted light. "Grow lights." With a flip of a switch the lights turned bright. "Sunlight." Then another click and it was dim. "There's also a watering system. Of course, everything's shut down now . . . has been for almost thirty years."

"I bet Sylvia would love to ride bikes with the kids. It would help take her mind off the situation outside. Give herself a chance to relax a bit."

Stuart recognized, all too well, the sound of despair in Katherine's voice. He also recognized her need to take care of her family in her own way. He admired her ability to cope with the unknown. He was surprised at the direction his thoughts had taken––he wanted to be there if she needed help.

Katherine turned back toward the door. "Let's go get them. It'll be fun––for all of us."

Stuart and Katherine entered the stable to find Gunner and Saint Nick with their tails tucked between their legs. They were both glued to Russ. Lizzie was further down the aisle watching over the horses.

"Hey, Boss. I don't know what's gotten into the horses. They're upset about something. Started pacing in their stalls and pawing." He bent down and patted the dogs. "Something's got these guys worried too."

Katherine stopped in front of Bella's stall. The big black mare was indeed upset as she snorted and pawed the ground. Scared enough, the giant could easily charge right through the front of her stall.

Stuart glanced down the row. "When did this start?"

"Just now!" he shook his head. "One minute they're content and eating and the next they're all riled-up." Just then all three looked at each other at the sound of an explosion and felt a vibration in the ground.

"What the hell was that?" Russ shouted.

Renee ran out from a room Katherine hadn't noticed before. "What the hell was that?"

"We need to get inside and check the cameras," Katherine added.

"I'll check on the kids," Renee said as she turned toward the inner door.

Stuart shook his head. "Not yet. I don't want to upset the others by rushing in there. You and Kate stay here. Try to settle the horses. I'm going outside."

He'd called her Kate. Her smile warmed her heart.

The large double doors opened just enough for Stuart to squeeze through. Katherine couldn't imagine what could have happened. She needed a plan if Stuart didn't come back. Would Russ know enough about the shelter to take care of them for however long it would take for this horror to end? But before she could formulate a plan the doors slid open and Stuart appeared unharmed.

"There's been a major explosion nearby. I'm not sure what, but it's to the north. There's a tower of black smoke along with flames. The blast was strong enough to take out that old dead maple up on the hill. One of the limbs rolled down just outside the door."

Katherine's legs turned to jelly. She sat down on the closest bale of hay. "I thought this was all over."

"What do you want me to do, Boss?"

"Stay here with the horses. They'll settle down if they see you're not afraid. Just act normal and reassure them that they're okay. Kate and I will take another look at the cameras and make some phone calls. I'll let you know what's up."

Katherine almost forgot their mission to get to the communication room without causing any alarm when she broke out laughing. Before them were all four children, riding bikes and tricycles in a circle around Sylvia on a pogo stick. The sight of her daughter-in-law bouncing up and down while desperately trying to maintain her balance on the two small footpads was just too much.

Sylvia glanced up. "It's a lot harder than I remember!" She nearly fell off. "You should come in and try it. You might as well have a little fun!"

Katherine waved her off and followed Stuart to the living room doorway. "He wants to show me something . . . we'll be right out!" She prayed she would have good news or at least no news when she and Stuart returned to join in the fun. It was obvious none of them had felt the ominous vibration, maybe because they were a good distance from the outer walls and separated by the stable.

Stuart stood before the TV screen. "What the hell?" He flipped switches. "The cameras were working just fine a few minutes ago." Katherine stood at his side looking at the blank screen. He flipped the switches again. "Shit! What the hell happened out there?"

This behavior, after hours of Stuart being totally calm and in control, sent cold shivers of fear racing through Katherine. "You're scaring me." She watched as Stuart smacked the top of the TV and waited for a picture to appear. "What's happening? Why is the screen all fuzzy?"

Stuart looked up as he continued flipping switches. "Shut the door."

She didn't like this new side of Stuart but quietly shut the door and returned to his side. "What happened?" She watched him pick up the telephone and listen. He slammed the phone back down.

"We've lost all communication with the outside."

15

Tunnels, 6:00 P.M.

Morgan gripped the Walther PPK with both hands, the way she'd been taught when she sat in for a week of FBI training, doing research for a story. Those semi-automatic handguns were bigger, heavier and packed a big punch. Her arms and wrists had hurt for weeks after. This petite little thing was amazingly lightweight, but it gave her at least a smidgen of confidence.

The four walked single file with Miguel in the lead. Stan and he had discussed the plan on how the four of them would get from the toy box to the Federal Reserve as quickly as possible without being seen. The fastest and most direct route would be under Superior, but that would mean they'd be in plain sight for the length of two blocks. Instead they'd follow Miguel in a roundabout way that would get them to the closest corner without detection.

Morgan followed Stan with Lamar behind. Her focus was as much on keeping her heels from contacting the cement floor and giving away their presence, as keeping up so Lamar didn't plow into her. Why hadn't she sent Naomi up to get the van keys from Jerry when she had the chance back at the office, since Lamar had proudly announced that he'd locked the van after grabbing her bag phone earlier? Her Nikes would feel real good now—so would her jacket. She was getting a charley horse from walking on her toes. Stupid. The alternative was to go barefoot—not an option. Suddenly Stan stopped and held out his arm. They had reached a corner.

A loud, raspy sounding voice echoed in the distance. Stan put his finger to his lips signaling everyone to remain quiet. He then changed places with Miguel and leaned as far forward as he could to listen.

"As soon as they get here, we'll blow the door!" The raspy voice was raised enough to be clearly heard.

"We should have been out of here by now!" It was the voice of a much younger man.

"No shit! Just what do you want me to do? The torch ain't enough to break that seal," said a gruff voiced man.

"Someone fucked up! This was to be a piece of cake! What if someone found out what we had stored in the mine and called the cops? Maybe we're in this alone!" This was a fourth man speaking with an accent.

"Shut up! The streets above are deserted, or didn't you notice! That means the plan is working!" said Raspy Voice.

"We're the part that isn't working! Now we have to fix it," shouted Mr. Gruff.

Stan motioned for Morgan to come forward. She tiptoed to his side, careful not to make a sound. "I think Mr. Gruff is the leader," Stan whispered. "I wish I could get a look at how many there are and what they're doing."

Miguel took a step forward to lean against Stan's back. "We can take 'em all now. They're fucked up! They won't know what hit 'em," he whispered in Stan's ear.

Stan shook his head. "Not yet," he whispered and motioned Miguel back while he continued to listen.

"How are they going to know we need more explosives to finish the job? We should be waiting at the loading dock by now!" This was the voice of the younger man and he was definitely nervous.

"Okay. You take someone with you, along with one of the carts, and head to the loading dock. When the others arrive, pile as many explosives and tools as you can on the cart and come back. Have the drivers stay with each of the ambulances and bring everyone else back with you. We need all the help we can get to load this stuff quickly. The explosion is going to rock the street. We want to be gone before the cops figure out what's happened," Mr. Gruff said.

"You idiot! What are you thinking?" Another raised voice, but this time he was older. "You put that much plastic around the door and we all go up in tiny pieces!" Something hit the floor with a muffled sound. "There's plastic and detonators in that bag. Don't wait for the others. We have to be out of the tunnel when that door blows! The sound alone will travel through every inch of these tunnels! It'll blow out our eardrums! I didn't spend months planning this operation for you to kill me!"

This guy definitely sounded educated. And understood explosives. Stan ran through in his mind what had been said so far. He hadn't heard enough to put a country to the accent, but the man was definitely the architect of the heist.

"Okay, you got a point." It was Mr. Gruff. "We'll move everyone far into the basement of the empty building and detonate from there. We'll have less than ten minutes to get the job done and be back to the loading dock and the ambulances. Then the place will be crawling with cops."

"What if someone catches on and tries to stop us?" said the kid.

"Yeah, right! Like who's going to see us down here?" Mr. Gruff was sounding much too confident and cocky.

It would be to their advantage if they could take them by surprise, thought Stan. And why wasn't Mr. Gruff or the Architect worried about blowing up what was on the other side of the door? It certainly wasn't jewels or artwork.

Morgan leaned against the tunnel wall with the Walther PPK held down at her side. She no longer cared about odors, dirt, or slime. It was all about the enemy and staying alive. She would dispose of every article of clothing that presently covered her body as soon as she walked through the door of her apartment. No, that wasn't correct.

She would have to get rid of them at the station before she even got into her car. She knew there would forever be the lingering scent of the tunnels on the cloth seats of her Chevy Impala. She made a mental note never to buy another car with cloth seats. Leather was definitely worth the added expense. Maybe it was time for a new car––a convertible. Morgan's thoughts were interrupted by a loud crash.

"Be careful, you idiot!" shouted Mr. Gruff. There was more arguing but she couldn't make out the words.

After the outburst, the tunnel went quiet again. Morgan assumed the bad guys were waiting for reinforcements to arrive. Her life was now in the hands of Miguel and Stan. Everything she'd learned in the last few hours about Stan told her she could trust him to protect her––even at the cost of his own safety––Miguel was another story. She prayed it wouldn't come to that. She prayed she wouldn't have to use her gun.

Stan motioned for everyone to move back down the tunnel.

It only took a couple of minutes for the four of them to reach the safety of the second tunnel. Stan brought everyone into a huddle, like a quarterback giving instructions for the next play.

"Listen, I think we may have our chance. These goons have run into a major problem. They can't get the door to the Federal Reserve open and remove the booty. Mr. Gruff thinks he needs the additional explosives in the ambulances. Two guys are taking a cart and heading to the loading dock. That means there will be just four guys left for us to deal with, and we have the added advantage of surprise."

Morgan shook her head. "They can't get in. Not even with explosives."

"Lady, you don't know what you're talking about. That door will blow into tomorrow!"

Morgan's eyes found Miguel's as she continued to shake her head. "Not if I'm right about what I saw––or maybe it's what I didn't see last year."

"Okay. Morgan, you better be right because you're putting our lives on the line. What else do you know about that building?"

Morgan motioned for Stan to follow her further down the tunnel, out of hearing range of the others. She shifted the tote bag to the other shoulder. "I wish I could sit down."

"Suit yourself. Miguel and I sit on the ground all the time. But whatever you do, times a-wasting."

She didn't sit. "I think I know what my guide was so upset about when he looked at the back wall. It was obvious by the open vault door that they were in the process of getting it ready for something. Maybe something bigger than anything that had come before, and they needed to reinforce the wall before it arrived——it's bombproof."

Stan's eyes searched Morgan's for any trace of doubt. "Okay we need to head back to the others.

Miguel lifted his gun. "I can take 'em all out. Then we pick off the others as they come back."

"And then we all go to prison." Stan glanced at each one. "I have a better idea."

16

Grand River, 6:00 P.M.

Once Michael was sure he was safe he turned on the generator, plugged in his mobile phone and punched in the number for the security office. Naomi filled him in on Morgan's theory about the explosions at the three nuclear power plants and everything that was happening in Lake County was a smokescreen for a heist at the Federal Reserve Bank. She mentioned how Sam was trying to get the authorities to stop the two ambulances before they got to Cleveland. After assuring Naomi that everything was fine with him, he hung up wondering what he should do next.

"Hey, Mike! You okay?"

Without looking up Michael recognized the voice of Scott Ferguson. They had been best friends since the third grade when the Fergusons moved to Painesville from Pittsburgh. Scott had enrolled in the police academy just after turning twenty-one and had recently become Fairport Harbor's youngest police chief.

Michael felt the boat tip as Scott climbed aboard. "Yeah, I'm okay. What the hell is going on?"

Scott leaned down to get a better look inside the cabin. "I can't believe you survived all that was going on. Those guys were shooting up the place but good!"

"You don't have to tell me. I watched them blow up the Coast Guard station!"

"Yeah, well, not exactly. Actually, the National Guard commander would like you to join us. I'm supposed to bring you in. He's holed up in my office while he puts this all together."

Michael grabbed his mobile bag phone and climbed the three steps to the deck. He slid the hatch cover into place and locked it.

The speedboat was still burning, the jeep had been abandoned across the river, and the Coast Guard Station, or what was left of it, was enveloped in a black cloud. He choked on the smell of burning rubber.

The short drive to the police station took only a few minutes. Michael focused on the flames and smoke coming from the direction of the Diamond Shamrock plant. Scott had to drive around a burning semi-trailer blocking the road.

"There's one of these at each of the streets leading out of town."

"Scott, what's going on? What happened?"

"You'll find out——soon enough."

These were the cause of the several smaller explosions he'd heard going off in succession. What caught Michael's interest even more, was that everything else in town looked normal, except for the crowds of people mingling around in groups along the streets.

Scott parked on the street in front of the station. He opened the door and got out. "Come on," he barked, then headed to the front door before Michael could ask what all the secrecy was about. Scott held the door as Michael entered the lobby. "Mike, this is Lieutenant Larsen. He's with the National Guard. He's in charge of this operation."

Michael glanced around the office. Except for the dispatcher, there wasn't another officer in the room, other than the man standing behind Scott's desk. "Thank you for coming Mr. Tanner. It appears you hold all the answers to what's been happening."

Michael shook the Lieutenant's outstretched hand. Although the words were casual Michael had an uneasy feeling in the pit of his stomach. Something just wasn't right.

"Sit down and tell me why you were on your boat today."

The question seemed unimportant. "I intended to overhaul the engine."

"Why did you choose to do it today? Why not during the week?"

"What does this have to do with anything?" Michael asked.

"Just answer the question, Mr. Tanner." The Lieutenant's tone was no longer casual.

"This was the only day I had free. The sporting goods store I own is closed on Sundays. My wife and sons were unpacking new merchandise. Why is this important? I thought you wanted to know about what happened."

"Do you deny that you were feeding false information to the television station and the Pentagon?" That uneasy feeling had suddenly turned to chilling fear.

Michael glanced over at Scott. He didn't seem surprised at the questions. "What *false* information? I was on my boat watching and reporting what was going on. And hopefully saving the lives of my family!"

"When did you first know there would be bombs planted outside of the three nuclear power plants?"

Michael placed both hands on the arms of the chair and prepared to get up. "I didn't know anything until my sister, Morgan, told me after hearing it from the station manager! Now, I'm leaving and going to look for my wife and sons!"

Lieutenant Larsen leaned forward. "You're not going anywhere Tanner, until I have the whole story––from the beginning."

Pentagon? Where did that come from? The nightmare wasn't over, and this guy was serious. "Okay, from the beginning. I had my head and shoulders in the bilge working on the engine. I first heard the noise and got up and looked out the hatch. Military jeeps were coming out of the salt mine, I thought the National Guard might be using the closed mine for training maneuvers. Then the one jeep stopped and faced the river and started shooting, blowing up the speedboat and shooting at a poor fisherman. I think he swam to Ram Island. Someone needs to see if he's all right. That's when I knew they weren't training. I closed the hatch cover and watched from inside. I stayed as still as I could so my boat wouldn't move. I didn't want the guy with the machine gun to start firing at me." Michael took a long steady breath. "I then called my sister, Morgan, and told her what I saw and she called her boss at the TV station."

"And *that* caused some major panic, Tanner!"

"Sorry, Lieutenant, but I didn't cause anything. Maybe it was those armed jeeps all heading in the direction of the Perry plant. Oh yeah, then there was the helicopter and all the explosions!"

"I assume, Tanner, that you knew the station manager was feeding this information to the local and state authorities."

"That's what I was hoping for. Shouldn't you be helping over at the Coast Guard Station? Did anyone make it out? I have buddies that may have been on duty."

"Everyone's fine and the boats are fine too."

It took a moment for this news to register in Michael's brain. His stomach twisted in knots with a, *Oh shit, this can't be happening* feeling. He looked at Scott then back to Larsen. "I don't understand. I heard the explosion and saw the smoke."

"And you reported what you *thought* you saw, which then went to the authorities. What *really* happened was that everyone on duty at the time of the shift change was knocked out with a gas. They were then taken to a nearby equipment storage garage. Everyone was tied up and given an injection that kept them unconscious for hours."

"But I saw the explosion––flames shooting above the treetops."

"You *heard* an explosion and saw the subsequent burning of a large pile of old tires!"

"What about the jeeps and the guard? They were definitely real."

Lieutenant Larsen leaned back in his chair. "We found them abandoned at the old Diamond Shamrock plant. The jeeps had recently been painted to appear military, the machine guns were real, and the helicopter is there as well."

Michael let out a long sigh. "So, why are you questioning me? It looks like you already know what happened. I hope you're looking for the ambulances."

"I want to know, Tanner, why and *how* you contacted the Pentagon?"

His body turned to ice in bone-chilling fear. "I just called my cousin, Travis Tanner, to see if he knew anything about this, or if he could find out what was going on. Turns out he only knew about the three power plant explosions."

The Lieutenant balled his fist and slammed it on the desk. "Then *how* did the Secretary of Defense *and* the Secretary of the Treasury get involved with this?" he shouted.

Michael flinched at Larsen's sudden, physical show of anger. He couldn't help but smile at the thought that *his* cousin had a pipeline to the top––he wondered if the President had been called. The mere idea warmed his heart enough to melt his fear.

"Tanner? I'm waiting." Larsen's voice vibrated with anger, his face glowed red.

Michael figured a straight answer would be best. "Travis and Richard Cheney are friends. I don't know about the Secretary of the Treasury. I have no idea what my cousin told them."

"You seem to have friends everywhere. What do you know about the salt mine?"

Michael glanced over at Scott for support, but he just shook his head. "It's been closed down while new equipment is put in place. I really don't know how or when all of those vehicles got in there. Or even where they came from." He was losing patience with this whole line of questioning––like he was some kind of spy or something. "Shouldn't someone over at the Coast Guard station, or maybe the police, have noticed that something really weird was going on?"

Larsen glared and continued. "What do you know about the Diamond Shamrock property?"

"Uh, Diamond Alkali was a huge, one thousand-acre facility that in its day resembled a small city. It was abandoned decades ago and is now nothing but a huge chemical dump. Land's dead––toxic. Like a commercial ghost town that no one will ever be able to live on." Michael had had enough of this bullshit. The interrogation was over. "This is all a huge waste of time! You should be trying to stop those ambulances!"

Scott moved to the side of the desk. "Mike's a good, decent guy. He only reported what he saw. He and his family are upstanding citizens. Maybe we should listen to him about those ambulances."

It took Michael less than ten minutes to inform Larsen and Scott of Morgan's theory. This could all be a smokescreen for something big happening in downtown Cleveland.

Lieutenant Larsen pounded the desk again as he jumped up from his chair. "Why the hell didn't you tell me this when you walked in here? We've wasted valuable time!"

Michael turned to Scott and rolled his eyes. After they got to the sidewalk Michael turned to his friend. "Now what are we supposed to do?"

"How about riding along with Pete? I've got him checking out the neighborhoods."

17

Royalwood, 6:45 P.M.

"**D**amn it! Somebody open the door!" A melody of chimes could clearly be heard from beyond the elegant black door. "Everyone else has a simple doorbell that rings once and stops." Michael pounded his fist a few more times. "This place has church bells!"

Officer Pete Porter leaned against the doorjamb. "There isn't anyone here! Yeah, the bells are loud which means that if there was anyone in *any* part of this house they would know we're out here."

"Pete, my family is around here somewhere! I'm sure Sylvie said they were at Royalwood. At least I *think* she said Royalwood." Michael pleaded.

"I've been watching. There isn't even a dog racing across the yard to check us out. And a place this big surely would have at least one dog."

Michael had grown up with Scott and Pete and the three had been as close as brothers. Maybe closer. Pete had been considerably overweight in elementary school and been called Tubby by most of the other kids who enjoyed tormenting him. But both Scott and Michael enjoyed the role of protector the first time a bully tried to push Pete into the whirling merry-go-round during recess. Over the summer break following the seventh grade, Pete had a growth spurt that continued for the next two years. By graduation, he was a tall string bean.

"Come on. Let's drive over and check out the stable." Pete pointed to a large white barn on the far side of a fenced pasture.

Michael was the first one out of the patrol car. He ran to the tall barn doors and slid the right side open. Soft rays of the evening sun streamed in through high windows and the nicker of horses greeted them.

"Wow! Pete said with a whistle. "There are people who don't live this well!"

Michael followed Pete down the long aisle lined with large stalls with brass-trimmed doors. Michael counted six black horses happily eating hay from corner feeders.

Pete reached his hand into one of the buckets scraping the bottom with his fingers. "What grain is left is dried on the bottom. They were last fed sometime this morning." He continued walking down the aisle. "There are six horses missing."

Michael stopped behind him. "How do you know that? And this isn't helping us find my family."

"There are six stall doors open, some grain left in the buckets and plenty of hay on the floor. I didn't see any horses in the pastures we passed, so they're not outside. If they're not in here or in a pasture, then they're not on the property."

Pete turned and followed Michael back up the aisle. "My guess is that Mr. Royal took six of his horses to a show. I've seen the Royalwood rig and it's huge. It can easily hold six of these big guys with room to spare. He'll probably return tonight."

Pete reached the doors when the dispatcher's voice came over the radio in the patrol car. Michael reached for the barn door's handle. "I'll get this. You answer the call."

The door slid easily on its track. Michael turned toward the car as Pete leaned out and yelled that they needed to go. "The chief wants me to check out that last big explosion site near here."

"What about my family? They have to be here! I'm sure that's what Sylvie said." Michael slid onto the seat and closed the door. "Can we at least stop at the other house near the road? It's probably the farm manager or someone connected to the property. They may know something."

"Look, Mike, I know you're worried. But you admitted yourself that the reception was so bad that you only caught bits and pieces of what was said. Maybe you got it wrong. And besides, the horse trailer isn't here, so that means no one else is here either."

"Okay. Maybe I'll come back later and check again."

They stopped in front of the bungalow on the way out.

"There's no one here either," said Pete. "The place looks locked up and, believe me if a manager of this estate was home, he would have been out here to flag us down."

"I agree," Michael sighed. "Let's go."

Pete stopped just past the gates to the estate to make the turn onto the main road. Michael glanced in his side mirror as the sun reflected off something shiny parked behind the barn.

"Hey, Pete. Turn around and go back. I think I see the trailer."

"I'm telling you they're not here. We need to move on. What was Sylvie driving?"

"A black Ford Explorer."

"Don't worry, we'll find them."

18

"*T*his is your plan?" Morgan asked, shaking her head. She wanted to slide down the grimy walls to the slimy floor below. She needed to sit. She needed to rest her chin on raised knees and wrap her arms tightly around them. She needed to get into a fetal position. She needed to be small and innocent and protected.

"It's the only way," said Stan, his voice lowered. "They're waiting for more explosives to arrive to blow the door. We can't let them do that. If that wall has been reinforced to withstand a bomb then an explosion could damage these tunnels, not to mention the adjoining buildings."

"Your plan is based on *chance* and *timely* communication! Neither of which is very reliable at the moment! So, the way I see this ending is . . . We all die," Morgan exclaimed in a hushed voice.

"Morgan, it's the *safest* way!"

"You're actually serious about putting the success of this operation in the hands of Naomi and Jerry? We're going to sit back and hope they can convince the police, or the National Guard, or whomever, to surround the building at the right moment and catch the bad guys?"

"What is your suggestion of how we should handle this?" Stan asked with more than a little sarcasm in his voice.

Morgan stared down at her ruined shoes, now more brown than black, her feet cold and wet. She didn't want to know what the wet, brown stuff might be. She let out a long sigh of frustration. "I don't know, but I sure don't want to put our lives in Jerry's hands. He might be good at taking direction, but he sure can't think on his feet!"

Stan raked the fingers of his right hand through his hair. "You're right, I'll go and make the calls."

Miguel spoke up for the first time. "No way, man! It'll take you too long to get all the way back to the tower. Shit. Anything can happen!"

"I'm just going to the phone closet. It won't take all that long. Besides, these guys still haven't figured out how to get the damn door open. They're way off schedule."

Morgan grabbed Stan's arm as he turned to leave. "Listen, Jerry isn't needed in the tower any longer. We already know where the ambulances are going and if we have Lamar watching the street and someone in the phone closet then we can still control what's happening and Jerry can help us down here."

Stan threw up his arms in a helpless gesture. "Come on! We don't have time to debate this here."

Morgan let Stan run on ahead of her. She didn't want to slow him down and arrived at the phone closet a minute later. She waited outside since there was only room for one person inside. She'd missed the beginning of the call, but didn't think it was anything important.

"I need you to get Jerry and the security guard back down to the office and have them wait until Lamar gets there. Lamar will give directions to the guard . . ." Morgan mouthed the name Mac. "Mac, on where to go and watch for the arrival of the ambulances. Lamar and Jerry will come here to us." Stan pulled Morgan to him and placed the phone between their ears so both could hear Naomi.

"I understand. I'm writing it down as we speak," Naomi said.

"Who are you talking to regarding law enforcement?"

"It's all going through Sam at the TV station. I think he's in touch with the various police departments, the National Guard and the Sheriff's Department. I talked to the Cleveland Police Chief, mostly about the boats."

Naomi's voice sounded calmer than it had earlier. That was good since Stan had a strong feeling that shit was going to hit the fan real soon. "Okay, this is important. There are to be *no* police cars anywhere in the vicinity of the Federal Reserve Bank until *after* the ambulances have gotten into place. I want these goons to feel that all is going as planned. Understand?"

"Yes. I've got it," Naomi said in a strong voice.

Stan was about to hang up when Morgan grabbed the phone. "Naomi, it's Morgan. Tell Jerry to bring all his equipment, including the light bar when he comes. Lamar can help him carry it. Thanks, talk to you later."

Stan turned to Morgan after closing the door to the closet. "Just what was that all about? Like we need more stuff to worry about."

"Listen, the cops know Jerry and I are here. Sam's been in touch with the authorities and so has Naomi and by now they know who is feeding the information. When the good guys arrive, they're going to expect to find us where the action is. That light bar can produce enough watts to blind those idiots. It may just help."

Stan pressed his hand on Morgan's back. "You do have a good point. Then you jump in and do your award-winning story."

Morgan turned her head toward Stan with a grin. "This is the biggest story to hit Cleveland in years. I intend to be the reporter that gets the exclusive. *And* I have my cameraman to document the takedown."

Stan stopped midstride and eyed Morgan from head to toe. "I know we're short on mirrors down here, but you really need to think about your appearance before going before the camera." He turned around and headed back down the tunnel.

Morgan focused on Stan's back as she tried to keep up.

He turned his head and glanced over his shoulder. "You might want to consider keeping it to headshots."

Morgan's first thought was to throw her tote bag at the back of his head. But then it would fall to the floor and land in the slime she still hadn't put a name to. Her favorite tote bag would have to follow her clothes into the trashcan.

The tunnel was quiet at the moment, the silence just broken by the soft click of Morgan's heels. Stan knew she was trying her best to walk as softly as possible and not bring them unneeded attention. He knew she was right about her and Jerry being in the tunnel when the authorities arrived. The problem was he and Miguel couldn't be seen. Two homeless guys on the streets would just blend in and get little more than terse words to move on. But down here it would become a major issue and there was also the problem of how to hide Commando Joe with an AK-47 wrapped around his neck. No, they had to be long gone and the guns safely locked up. He and Miguel would have to disappear.

19

Flames raced heavenward, dancing in and around the plume of black smoke. Michael kept his eyes on the fire as Pete drove toward the fire truck. Chief Connors jogged toward them waving his arms for them to stop. "Better not come any closer. That wall could go anytime. This is a bad one!" He leaned against the patrol car to catch his breath. "We can't get this under control. We've been fighting it for over an hour." He took another deep breath. "Keep getting secondary explosions."

"What would cause it to reignite like that?" Pete asked as he watched another smaller truck park next to the edge of the lake just beyond. Two men jumped out and began dragging a large hose toward the water.

"The first explosion blew out the back wall but contained the fire. There must have been another, bigger fuel tank we didn't know about." Chief Connors nodded in the opposite direction. "The second explosion sent fuel oil and gasoline across the field beyond. The wind is pushing the fire in the direction of that farmhouse on the other side."

Pete craned his neck to get a better look. "So, you gonna use the water from the lake to contain the field? Good call. Trucked in water has to be getting pretty scarce right about now."

"Yeah. All of Chardon's, Chesterland's and Mentor's equipment is in Painesville and Fairport."

Michael shook his head in disbelief as he watched the firefighters scrambling to hook up the hoses to the truck.

"The owner is on his way over now. Apparently, the company in Chardon who owns this place uses it to store equipment. They took in a large delivery of paint and had both the oil and gasoline tanks filled last week."

"Any idea how it started?" Michael asked.

"I think you want to talk with the lady in the farmhouse. She's the one who called it in. I need to get back to the rig. This isn't going to slow down any time soon."

Pete backed the patrol car out of the lot and headed toward the house. "This side of the house looks like it took the worst of a gang war. All the windows look broken."

"No place was safe anywhere close to this. Sylvie and the kids could have taken shelter in an innocent-looking house like this. We're not all that far from Royalwood or Oakwood property. I'm sure they felt an explosion as big as this one." Michael's fear for his family came through in a fevered pitch. "They could be trapped in a building somewhere!"

Pete patted Michael's shoulder. "Don't be thinking the worst. Sylvie and your mother are both women who can take care of themselves. Don't forget, they have Gunner and Saint Nick with them. They would have found a safe place."

Michael wasn't so sure.

Pete parked in front of the steps of the two-story Victorian farmhouse. Singed paper covered the yard in a blanket of white. "Looks like the explosion might have taken out a file cabinet or two."

A woman appearing to be in her late thirties stood on the porch. Three young children crouched at her side with arms wound tightly around her legs.

"I'm officer Porter and this is Michael Tanner. I understand from the fire chief that you saw what happened."

The woman nodded and motioned for them to follow her into the house. The two rooms on the left side of the house were open to each other. Just a low wall containing built-in cabinets with leaded glass doors to divide what looked like a living room and dining room. Broken glass covered the floor and furniture. Air, heavy with the acrid sting of smoke hung around them.

"Come on, we can talk in the kitchen."

Pete noticed the wedding ring and was glad to see she was married. "Is your husband home?"

"He's on his way back. He's a carpenter and went to pick up sheets of plywood. I'm taking the kids to my parent's house on the West side of Cleveland later tonight."

"Good idea. There are roadblocks in the worst-hit areas so I would head directly south from here where there was less activity. You should be fine."

Michael leaned against the counter. "Can you tell us what happened?"

"It was scary enough with the explosions and a helicopter flying around. Chet, my husband, was saying we should head down to the basement. The kids were hungry, so I started making sandwiches to take down with us. Chet grabbed some drinks from the fridge. He'd been watching that helicopter. All the explosions seemed far away. He said we'd be okay but should stay in the basement anyway. Chet's real good about taking care of us." She moved to the kitchen table where her children sat with coloring books. "Do you have kids?" She asked Pete.

"Yes, I do. Three girls." Pete waited until her focus was once again on him. "What happened next?"

"All of a sudden the sound of whirling blades got louder and I went to the window. The helicopter was coming right toward the house. Chet and I grabbed the kids and headed for the basement. I didn't even take the sandwiches––or my keys––or my purse." She hesitated. "I should have remembered to keep them near me. I wasn't thinking straight."

"Had it come close before that?" Pete asked.

"What?" She glanced back at the kids. "No. When we got to the bottom of the stairs an explosion rocked the house. There was breaking glass. I could hear things hitting the floor. The kids were screaming. I thought we were going to die. I sat on the floor and held the kids in my lap. It wasn't long before the sound moved away. When we couldn't hear it any longer Chet came upstairs. He yelled down that there was a fire. I brought the kids upstairs and called the fire department."

Michael glanced out the window. "It looks like they're getting the field under control."

"Do you have kids, Sir?" She asked Michael.

"Two boys. I wish I knew where they are. If they're safe."

She gave Michael a look like he was the worst, most deplorable man on earth for not protecting his family.

Michael wasn't about to go into the events of his day with this woman. Her life was tragic enough without hearing about his. He pursed his lips in anger––anger at himself for not knowing where Sylvie and the boys were. He should be out there, in the fields, searching. Silently he pleaded with his buddy to continue.

Pete pulled a spiral notebook and pen from his breast pocket. "Did you hear a whistling sound before the explosion?" Pete flipped open the cover and began writing. "Or maybe machine gun fire?"

"No, just the sound of the helicopter getting closer and then the explosion."

"How long were you in the basement?"

"I don't know. I was terrified. I just don't know."

"I'm sorry, ma'am, but can you think of anything else that you might have heard?"

"No. It all happened so fast."

Pete slipped the notebook back into his pocket. "Thanks for your help. Will you be okay until your husband gets home?"

"We'll be fine. He should be here soon."

Back in the patrol car Michael turned toward his friend. "You thinking it could have been some kind of rocket fired from the helicopter?"

"I really don't know. It sounds possible based on what she said was happening. Being this close, she should have heard some kind of missile before it hit. A bomb would have left the structure nothing more than a pile of rubble. Whatever it was, it sure did a number on that building!"

Pete turned the car around and headed down the drive. "How about we check out the Oakwoods's parking lots and see if there's a black Explorer. Then we head back to Fairport."

"Now you're talking––Tubby." Both men laughed at Michael's use of Pete's childhood nickname. Somehow thinking of their younger years seemed to make the moment less tragic.

20

S tan slowed his pace so Morgan could keep up. On his own, he could have been back to Miguel's location minutes ago, but the poor thing was nearly jogging on her toes so the heels of her shoes wouldn't make unnecessary noise. She held her tote bag tightly against her side to prevent it from flapping––again, preventing unnecessary noise. He didn't know of another woman who would have endured what she had since entering the tunnels and running into two homeless men without whining and complaining. Sure, she'd probably walk across alligators if it meant getting a Pulitzer. He had to give her credit––the woman had guts. He fantasized about helping Morgan out of those horrid smelling clothes––until Miguel ran toward them holding the rifle against his chest.

"Where the hell you been man? Shit's comin' down and I can't see around the fuckin' corner. One of 'em's asking for more plastic."

Stan glanced over his shoulder at Morgan. "You got a mirror in that bag of yours?"

Morgan pulled the tote down in front of her as they walked. "Yeah, a small one." After rummaging through the many small items on the bottom she came up with the mirror and flipped open the cover.

Stan knelt at the corner as Morgan handed him the mirror. "Stand back and be ready to run if they see me." He didn't like this one bit. He was forced to rely on the authorities to make this takedown happen and that didn't sit well. Adjusting the mirror up and down he finally got the image he was looking for. Three men were in sight. One was pressing the plastic explosive around the perimeter of the steel door. A second was handing him more from a sack held by the third who was standing off to the side. From the few words he could make out, the general consensus was they should be adding more explosives. Years of military experience with explosives told him these idiots didn't know what the hell they were doing. More was not better and they could all die. There was also the real possibility they could be faced with a cave-in that would cause massive damage to the tunnels, the streets above, and the adjoining buildings. He had to stop them before they detonated. Stan figured he had a few minutes while the guys exited the tunnel and took cover in the basement of the empty building.

Miguel leaned down. "What's happenin'?

Stan handed the mirror back to Morgan. A soft rustling sound coming from further back in the tunnel drew his attention. He let out a sigh of relief as Lamar and Jerry came into view. "Glad you're here. We need to move fast and stop this now. Jerry, start unpacking your gear and be ready to move into place and hit the lights."

Lamar handed Morgan a pair of sneakers and her jacket with the WJW-TV logo on the front. "We stopped at the truck first to get the light bar. Jerry thought you could use these."

"Thanks." Morgan leaned against Lamar for support while kicking off a shoe, then shoved her foot into the Nike. He was as sturdy as a brick wall. She repeated the process, bent down to quickly tie the laces then slipped into the warm jacket.

Lamar kicked the slime-covered shoes against the wall. "I'll come back tomorrow––the next time those see daylight will be in a trash bin."

Morgan's chest tightened, she struggled to keep her breathing even. She'd never, in her whole life, been this scared. But she couldn't let Stan see the fear pushing her into the shadows of the dimly lit tunnel. It was up to her and Jerry to stop these men before they got any further in their plan and stole whatever it was on the other side of the door. After all, this was her doing. It was her need to track down the story behind the two boats at the East Ninth Street pier. And it was her need to prove herself as a reporter capable of doing more than human-interest stories that got her and Jerry into this mess.

She looked up into Stan's eyes, now steel-gray and unwavering. He believed in the plan and she wouldn't let him down. She probably would never see him again after she and Jerry took their places center-stage. But she wanted to. She'd felt a connection right from the beginning––the deep tone in his voice sent sexual vibrations to parts of her body she couldn't think about––at least not with a homeless man. He'd opened up to her about his time in Nam and the obligation he felt toward Miguel. She, too, had put her life in his hands without doubting him for a minute. Morgan wished she could stop time––it was too soon to say goodbye. Stan and Miguel would have to disappear before the authorities arrived on the scene. She took a deep breath and nodded. She was ready.

The beeper on Lamar's belt vibrated. "That's the signal. The cops are surrounding the area and moving in on the loading dock."

Stan took Morgan's hand and squeezed. "You okay?" he whispered.

Morgan nodded. "Yeah."

"Okay, people. It's showtime!"

Morgan and Jerry eased into position in the center of the tunnel. Lamar stood behind them with the light bar raised above his head. He flipped the switch. The powerful lights flooded the space in front of them startling the men as they continued packing the plastic explosives around the door.

Morgan raised the microphone close to her mouth. "I'm Morgan Tanner under the streets of Cleveland, Ohio. You are watching as these men are in the process of breaking into the Federal Reserve Bank."

Shouting suddenly erupted from further down the tunnel. She watched as one of the men reached down to the floor. "Where the hell are the guns?"

"I put them in the duffle bag. They're on the other cart." He started running toward the door leading into the vacant building.

Morgan glanced to her left where Stan and Miguel were waiting. She gave a quick nod, letting them know that she and Jerry weren't in danger. The bad guys had misplaced their guns.

Stan winked and blew a kiss. Then the two men took off running toward the closest door that would lead them above ground.

Morgan turned her head back to the action before them. "We believe these are the same men who are responsible for the explosions outside of the three nuclear power plants and the explosions in Fairport Harbor and along the Grand River."

Just then doors burst open and the tunnel was filled with uniformed police and several men in dark-colored suits.

"It appears the authorities arrived just in time to prevent the explosives from being detonated and blowing the door of the Federal Reserve Bank. We don't know what lies beyond those walls. Whatever it is, it's valuable enough that this elaborate plan, crossing three states, and terrorizing Lake County, was put into action."

Morgan reached out the microphone so the voices beyond could be heard.

"You're seeing this as it happens. The men who have literally stopped our lives for the last seven hours are being taken into custody."

One of the men in a dark suit marched toward Morgan shielding his eyes from the blinding light. "Cut the lights! Who the hell are you and what are you doing down here?"

A sudden jolt of adrenalin raced through Morgan's body. This was her chance to shine, although the bright lights streaming over her right shoulder did little to warm her senses. She prayed her voice would hold strong and clear and not give away the doubt still gnawing at her confidence.

Morgan flipped the switch that turned off the microphone and motioned for Lamar to kill the lights. She maintained eye contact with the suit strutting toward her. "Who am I? *I'm* Morgan Tanner, with WJW-TV news. The reason I'm standing here covered in unmentionable slime is because I'm the one who blew the whistle on this little shindig. And *who* exactly, are you?"

"Special Agent McGuire." He craned his neck and looked around her to see down the side tunnel. "I was told we had informants down here feeding us information."

Morgan relaxed. This guy had no clue what was happening. He was just following orders and apprehending the bad guys. She needn't be afraid. After all, she was the one holding all the cards––or the microphone. She was the reporter with the story at the front of national news. This was her show.

"That, Special Agent McGuire, would be *us*. Jerry, my cameraman, was the first to see that something was amiss when he noticed the two Sea Rays offloading the motorized carts and tarps."

"That doesn't explain what you're doing down here. You could have been killed."

"Just doing my job. Following the story. You guys never would have connected the dots without my help. You'd still be running around in circles in Lake County and the bad guys would have gotten away with the loot. By the way, what is *the loot*?"

Agent McGuire took hold of Morgan's arm. "The three of you are coming with me. You have a lot of answering ahead of you."

Morgan pulled her arm free. "Not until we finish down here. Now you get out of our way so I can finish this story. This is going to hit the National news. Do you want to be the one to stop that?"

Morgan watched his expression of bravado change to a frown of doubt.

"I thought so. Now follow me and if you're smart, you'll cooperate."

Morgan led the way to the steel door of the Federal Reserve Bank and positioned herself to the side. Lamar turned on the lights and Jerry nodded that he was recording.

"This is the door that was supposed to be blown to pieces, giving access to the valuable treasure beyond. You can see the plastic explosive that was packed in and ready for detonation. It was our arrival in the tunnel at the exact moment that the police and FBI arrived that prevented this horrific explosion. An explosion that could have severely damaged adjacent buildings and the street above."

Morgan paused and turned to her left. "Here with me is Special Agent McGuire of the Federal Bureau of Investigation." She placed the microphone in front of him as Jerry turned the camera. "Can you give us a picture of what would have happened if we hadn't gotten here in time to stop this?"

"This much explosive material would have caused extensive damage to the adjoining buildings and probably killed or critically injured everyone down here." He handed the mic back to Morgan with a scowl.

"Thank you. Although an elaborate and well-orchestrated plan, the wrong person was put in charge of blowing the door. And I can tell you, for a fact, that nothing can penetrate that wall and gain access to the room on the other side. The Federal Reserve Bank building is very well protected."

Morgan bent down and opened the duffel bag that had been left behind by the police and FBI agents. "Here is the bag containing the plastic explosives." She gently pulled the sides apart to give Jerry a better view. "As you can see there is plenty more that wasn't used." From another bag, she pulled out a handful of small objects with wires attached and gave them to Special Agent McGuire. "Do you know what these are? There seems to be quite a few."

The agent took a long look then nodded. "Detonators for the plastic explosive."

"How many would have been needed to blow this door?"

"Just one."

Morgan turned toward the opposite wall. "Now, follow me and we'll enter the basement the criminals used as their escape route."

They stopped inside the door. "Here are the motorized carts that were to take the treasure to the loading dock of this vacant building. You can still see the stacks of canvas bags that would have held the items."

Morgan lifted one of the bags showing how large it was. "Obviously, whatever they were after, there was a lot of it." She then continued toward a large overhead door open to the outside. "Now for the get-away cars! Or––to be more specific––ambulances."

The camera continued to roll on the swarm of police and FBI agents who were still standing around the two ambulances and the numerous cars parked at all angles with flashing lights. Morgan then placed herself before the camera.

"This is what we believe happened to lead us to this point. Late this morning an explosion shut down the Davis Besse Nuclear Power Plant outside of Toledo. That was quickly followed by one at Palisades in Michigan and Nine Mile Point in New York. Everyone assumed that the Perry Nuclear Plant was next when Jeeps outfitted with machine guns began streaming out of the temporarily closed salt mine in Grand River. Buildings began exploding along the route to the Perry Nuclear Power Plant and various other areas of Lake County. Even a helicopter could be seen circling while structures exploded in its wake."

McGuire moved to take the camera from Jerry. "Enough!"

"Oh no, Special Agent McGuire, our audience needs to hear the rest." Morgan moved closer to the edge of the loading dock. "But you see, it was all just a case of smoke-and-mirrors––a means to take our attention away from what they were really doing here, in the tunnels under the city of Cleveland. They abandoned the Jeeps for ambulances and headed here to the loading dock of a building that has been empty for years. The bags would have been loaded and off they'd go. Who would question two ambu-lances leaving the city? Perhaps hooking up with a semi or maybe a plane?"

Morgan moved to the side next to Agent McGuire. She thrust the mic to his lips. "What were they after, Special Agent McGuire? Gold bars, maybe? They would certainly fit in these bags." He pushed the microphone away. "We may never know what lies beyond the wall that was worth a diabolical plan crossing three states. But we do know that it will go down in the history books as one of the most daring. I'm Morgan Tanner in Cleveland, Ohio."

The camera panned over the ambulances now covered in the orange glow of a setting sun. Morgan caught a glimpse of a dark form huddled in the doorway across the street. She didn't need to see a face to know it was Stan. She wished she could give him some sign that everything was good. Agent McGuire took the microphone from Morgan's hand and tossed it to Jerry. "You're in more trouble than you could ever imagine, lady. Pack up your gear!"

Morgan bent down to help Jerry fill the duffle bag. He leaned close to her ear and whispered. "What are we going to do now?"

Morgan took a long deep breath and thought about everything that had happened. She couldn't have done this without Stan and Miguel's help. She didn't know their story or why they needed to call the tunnels home. But what she was certain of was that she couldn't involve them in what was surely to become a very thorough FBI investigation. She glanced over to the doorway––he was gone.

Morgan looked at Jerry with what she hoped was a grin of confidence. "We lie. We never saw Stan or Miguel. We figured this out with the help of Lamar and Naomi. Yeah––we lie."

"Hurry it up! We're going to my office. I want a full report of how you got involved in this."

Morgan stood and faced McGuire. "Sorry. You're the one who will be coming with us to the station. We have just enough time to get this footage ready for the late-night news." She bent down and grabbed the tripod. "Then, after a new lead-in is taped and added to the front-end for National coverage, we'll be able to sit down and have our little chat."

An hour later, a dozen people stood in the TV studio, all focused on the news desk. The station manager gave Morgan the thumbs up. "That's a wrap, people. Nice job, Morgan."

"Thanks, Sam."

"Special Agent McGuire, you can use the Conference Room for your meeting with Morgan and Jerry. The phones are lighting up like

Christmas trees with calls coming in. It looks like I'll be in my office for the next several hours."

The news director approached as Agent McGuire's pager went off. "Morgan, I just got word that the network wants to break into the regular programming to air the story. CBS Chicago wants to do a live interview with you for their ten o'clock news. I imagine we'll be hearing from the rest of the country before the hour's up."

"I guess our interview will have to wait until tomorrow. I've been called back to my office." Agent McGuire gave no indication of the cause of the urgency, but the deep frown and scowl said a lot.

"Before you go . . . can you tell me what these guys were after?" Morgan asked.

"No."

"The public needs to know what this was all about. It's going to come out sooner-or-later."

McGuire turned to leave then stopped and glared over his shoulder. "I don't know!" He took a few steps then turned back with a helpless look. "I wish to God someone would tell *me* what's behind that damn wall."

21

Fairport Harbor 7:30 P.M.

The old abandoned Diamond Shamrock buildings were a smoldering pile of bricks and steel against a twilight sky, except one––the largest. A helicopter sat silently next to the building. They parked alongside the other police cars from Fairport, Grand River and Painesville. The National Guard vehicles were parked near the entrance with other emergency vehicles lined up along Fairport Nursery Road.

Michael glanced around the immediate area. Not a soul in sight. "Everyone must be inside that building."

"So, lets go!" Pete shouted and took off running.

It only took a minute for Michael and Pete to reach the open doors of the huge brick building. The scene before them caused both men to stop dead in their tracks.

"What the hell?" Pete saw Scott Ferguson standing to the right of the door. "You mean the jeeps were just left in here?"

"Looks that way," said Chief Ferguson as he walked toward them. "We're going over them now. See if they left anything behind. These buildings were the site of the last and largest explosion."

Michael raked fingers through his hair. "But I heard a huge explosion coming from here two hours ago. How can this be the last?"

"What you heard was a commercial propane tank going up."

"These guys went to a lot of trouble creating enough terror to shut down cities. Then leave their transportation in an abandoned building for the authorities to find?" Michael shook his head. "This just isn't making any sense."

"We're pretty confident we'll find fingerprints. Someone had to leave something behind——even a gum wrapper. We'll get these guys. Whoever they are."

A woman, on her hands and knees, checked the underside of the nearest jeep. Suddenly she jumped to her feet. "Bomb!"

A dozen officers raced for the doors. Michael and Pete were the first ones out. They stood at a safe distance at the perimeter of the abandoned plant. It only took seconds for everyone to clear out of the building after hearing the word bomb. All vehicles and personnel were now at a safe distance waiting for whatever came next.

Pete leaned against the front grill of the patrol car. "Let's head back to the station. Nothing's going to happen here until the bomb squad's finished——or this place blows. And who knows how long that's going to be. They could be almost anywhere in the county."

The air hung heavy with the biting smell of smoke, sirens could still be heard in all directions and the tension in the car was so thick it threatened to wrap its strong fingers around Michael's throat.

"I can't take this any longer! I've got to find my family!"

"And just where are you going to go? We've already checked the obvious places in and around the Botanical Gardens. I say we go back to the station and monitor what's happening, and you can make phone calls from a desk instead of driving all over the countryside. And besides, that bag phone of yours is next to worthless out here. Any signal you're lucky enough to get fades in and out."

"Yeah, you're right," Michael said with a defeated sigh.

The prevailing westerly winds pushed the smoke from the burning tires in Grand River right over Fairport Harbor. The nauseous fumes crept under doors and seeped in around old windows, filling the station with an eye-burning haze. Every time the front door opened a new cloud rushed in to add to the acrid stench.

Twenty minutes later Pete returned to the desk that Michael was using to make calls. He set a cup of black coffee in front of Michael and sat down in the chair opposite.

"Thanks," Michael said as he picked up the mug. It too smelt burnt.

Pete leaned back in the chair. "I just had an interesting conversation with the Chief of Staff of Lake East. The hospital has been on emergency stand-by all afternoon expecting massive numbers of casualties. The only people to arrive by ambulance so far are accident victims trying to get out of town, a few hit by flying glass or debris and one heart attack. Our dispatcher has logged in hundreds of calls. Most of them are asking what to do or reporting seeing the jeeps."

A frown deepened across Michael's brow. He shook his head. "With those jeeps driving around shooting off rounds from machine guns, I would have expected numerous gunshot victims."

"Not a one so far." Pete inched forward in his chair. "Except for the two we know about. Whoever was driving the speedboat that blew up, and anyone else who might have been on-board. There was also the poor soul who you saw gunned down while running across the parking lot at the salt mine.

"What about all the buildings that exploded?" Michael asked in a bewildered voice. "Maybe they were using some kind of rocket launcher. You know, the ones you see in the movies where the guys carry them around on their shoulders. Those could blow up buildings."

"We won't know for sure until the sites cool down and the FBI can search through the rubble. The biggest explosions were at the Diamond plant and that could take days to sift through. One thing we do know for sure is that they're no longer in the area."

Michael nodded in agreement. "Yeah, I was just talking to Naomi at the Terminal Tower. She's packing up and waiting for a couple guys named Lamar and Mac to let her know she can head home. She said Morgan and Jerry are good and ready to break the story––not sure what that means. The authorities have surrounded the building and taken everyone into custody. She thinks it may be over."

"What about Morgan? Is she okay? I hope she isn't doing anything dangerous." Pete lifted his eyebrows and tilted his head as if conjuring up a memory. "Remember when we were kids——she could *always* be found in the middle of any raucous activity?"

"I'm sure Morgan's fine. She's a reporter that gets all the easy fluff jobs. She'll step in when the fighting's over and report the take-down while looking as lovely as ever."

"You're right. Do we know yet what those goons were after? Has to be huge. Like a room full of gold bars."

"Not a clue. I agree it's gotta be worth orchestrating this kind of operation. I tried calling Mom's house and no-answer. No answer on the mobile either. My whole family's just disappeared. I can't take much more of this waiting!"

"You do know there was never any danger to the three nuclear plants? No radiation leaks. The explosions were all at the fence-lines." Pete paused. "Your family, up near Besse, are fine."

"Yeah. I know. But I can't rest until I find Mom, Sylvie and the kids."

"It's still too soon to be racing around the countryside. I've checked in with the Highway Patrol. Neither your mom nor Sylvia went through any of the roadblocks. They're logging in the license plate numbers of everyone who exits the county. So that means they're still somewhere close and we'll find them. Your mom's a tough old bird." Pete chuckled. "Trust me. She has this under control."

Michael pushed away from the desk. "I'm going back to the Royal's farm. Maybe someone's there now."

"Stay put. I had the helicopter pilot make another sweep of the property. There's no sign that anyone's there." Pete didn't want to worry Mike any further by telling him the horse trailer was seen parked behind the barn. But it worried him, and he was fresh out of answers for his friend.

"Okay, but I'll swing by on my way home."

"No need. I gave instructions to the pilot to add *Royalwood* to his search zone. He'll be in the air all night. If there's any sign that someone's on the property he'll call me." Pete stood. "I need to get back to the phones. Maybe just go home and see if Sylvia calls you."

Michael nodded his head in agreement. "Yeah. I think I'll go home. Call if you need me to help with anything."

"I'm going to finish up here and head back out to the Diamond plant. The bomb squad should be cleaning up. It's getting dark and there's a lot of ground to patrol. The real work starts tomorrow. I'll keep in touch. Let me know when you hear from Sylvia and your mom."

Michael stood and shook his friend's hand. "Thanks for all your help. At least I know that Morgan's safe."

22

Katherine moved to Stuart's side in the communication room. "Can you fix it? Maybe it's just a loose wire somewhere."

"These phone lines are almost forty years old. All of this electronic equipment was installed by my son and his friends." Stuart waved his hand over the table. "I wouldn't know where to begin."

Katherine took a moment to think. "Well, maybe if we figure out what went wrong, we can fix it."

"I think the explosion knocked out the wires up on the hill. An old tree came down. One of the large limbs rolled in front of the door." Stan slapped his hand against his leg. "I should have had that dead tree taken out years ago. I never thought it mattered any."

"Don't beat yourself up. You couldn't see into the future. I never worry about dead trees coming down––unless the house is in danger."

Stuart looked down with a smile. "Thank you, Kate." Her heart did a flip-flop.

"Can you send Russ out to check? Maybe it's nothing bad."

"Not in the dark. We'll need to wait till morning."

"How about our mobile phones. We've been charging the batteries. Couldn't we go outside and try to make calls?"

Stuart put an arm around Kate's shoulders. "I'm sorry. This is just one of those quirky places on the property that doesn't get reception."

Katherine gave a sigh of defeat. "I know. We couldn't get a signal at the cabin either."

"We need to stay here for the night, then Russ and I will go to the house first thing in the morning and make calls. If all goes as planned, we'll be back in time for breakfast."

"Sounds good." Katherine was glad she no longer had to be the one to come up with the answers to the mounting problems.

Stuart opened the door and motioned for Katherine to proceed. "Let's see what the others are up to. I think we should keep this little problem to ourselves."

Two hours later, Stuart turned down the patio lights to the dusk setting. The children were finally yawning and showing signs they were ready for bed. After all, spending the night in the shelter was just another part of the adventure.

Renee returned from the storage room with an armload of bedding. "Sylvia, how about you and me bunk with the kids? There's another room next to the kitchen that Katherine can use."

Half an hour later all was quiet. Katherine sat at the small table on the patio. The lights in the ceiling took on the magic of a star-filled night sky.

Stuart approached holding two glasses. "I thought we could both use a glass of wine. There wasn't much of a selection, just what Renee brought for dinner."

Katherine took a sip as Stuart sat down in the chair opposite. "Hmm, a light merlot. I don't think I could have handled a heavy cabernet. You would have had to peel me off the table."

Stuart watched the dark red liquid swirl around the side of the long-stemmed glass. "Were you thinking about the safety of your son and daughter? You had a faraway look when I approached."

Katherine inhaled deeply. "Actually, I was thinking about all of us, and how we were thrown into this unimaginable situation. The last time I talked to Michael he assured me he was fine and not to worry. Morgan is keeping in touch with the station, and as far as I know is just reporting on the events in Cleveland. She's in no danger at all and far removed from the action." She looked up and smiled. "And we're here safe and sound and having an adventure of our own."

They tipped their glasses in a silent salute, each in their own thoughts.

It was Katherine who spoke first after watching the frown deepening across Stuart's brow. "Something else is bothering you. Care to share?"

"I was wondering how my Aunt Lovinia is making out. I tried to call her earlier but there was no answer at the house. She's ninety years old and bedridden."

"Does she live in the area?"

"About a mile away, it's called *Royal's Leap*. Our properties join to the south. Her house is rather secluded so there aren't many neighbors who would know to look in on her. Besides, I think everyone is pretty much trying to take care of their own families. She has the farm manager who watches over the place. She isn't the easiest person to live with so housekeepers don't last more than a month or two."

Katherine set her glass down and leaned forward, resting her elbows on the table's edge. "I'm so sorry. You don't need another helpless person to worry about."

Stuart chuckled. "Lovinia Fairchild is anything but helpless!"

"What a beautiful name. Is she a Royal too?" Katherine did a slight nod. "I've seen the name *Royal's Leap* etched in a stone column. Rather intriguing––mysterious."

Stuart took a sip of wine before continuing. "She's my father's older sister. Quite a bit older and quite the character," he chuckled. "The name *Royal's Le*ap ties into early settler's lore. It's a romantic and tragic story––a story for another time.

Lovinia's story would take hours to tell. Stuart only had time for the shortened version. "Her father doted on her and she could do no wrong. She was already well into her teens when my father came along. She ran with a fast crowd that included some Broadway actors and musicians."

"So, I take it that with a son to carry on the Royal name your grandfather's attention shifted to your father."

"Yep, my father had to live up to the Royals' expectations while Aunt Lovinia was free to live her carefree life. She followed her friends to Broadway and became an actress. She was born Lavinia Royal, but she thought it sounded too sweet. So, before her first Broadway play she legally changed it to Lovinia––exaggerating the Lo. It sounded more dramatic. She wasn't a very good actress, but money buys a lot. It bought her a husband too. He was a respectable friend of the family who turned a blind eye to the fact that she was known to show more than long legs in black tights."

Katherine leaned back in her chair. "Does she have children that help take care of her?" It only seemed logical to Katherine that she would.

"She has a son who lives in New York. We see him and his daughter at weddings and funerals, but that's about it. I think there's some bad blood between mother and son. Not sure what. I guess she just drove him away too."

"Wow! I'd love to meet her. Sounds like quite the character."

Stuart swallowed the last of his wine. "Not much chance of that. I hear she's pretty much on her deathbed."

Any further discussion of Aunt Lovinia ended with the opening of the stable door.

"Hey, Boss. Renee and I will bed down with the horses for the night. I just need to grab our sleeping bags."

"You're going to sleep with the horses?" Katherine asked as if Russ had just lost his mind.

"Not literally. There's a small bunkroom. Sleeps four."

Russ moved closer. He bent down so only Stuart and Katherine could hear. "I took a chance and went outside. I didn't see the helicopter, but I heard it. Sounds different––bigger at night. Saw some kind of light, like the pilot was looking for something––maybe to shoot at.

There's a strong smell of smoke and the orange glow of something burning to the north. Lots of sirens in the distance."

Katherine took a moment to gather her thoughts. "What's going on? Do you suppose it was the helicopter that caused the explosion and took out our communications? I can't imagine how scared we would have been in that tiny cabin. This has to end tomorrow. Someone has to stop this. Where's our military?"

Stuart pushed his chair back and stood. "I'm sure we'll have answers tomorrow. I'll join you in the bunk room." He glanced over at Katherine. "You can have my bed for the night."

Katherine was too overwhelmed by the day's events to argue about sleeping arrangements. "Okay, I'll take your bed, but only if you agree to take my sleeping bag."

Half an hour later Katherine snuggled beneath a down comforter. As hard as she tried, she couldn't relax enough to fall asleep. Still worried about everyone else, she got out of bed and grabbed a quilt off a chair. Wrapping it around her shoulders, she padded to the bedroom assigned to the kids. Peeking inside, her eyes adjusted to the lack of light. Sylvia lifted her head giving a sign that all was well. Renee was sound asleep with her children tucked on either side. Saint Nick and Lizzie were curled up together in the middle of the room.

Katherine made her way back to the patio and sat down at the table staring at the stable door. She wanted to check on the men as well––she wouldn't be able to sleep until she knew that *everyone* was tucked in. She'd feel terrible if they were disturbed on account of her insomnia. Stuart and Russ had had a horrific day, they needed undisturbed sleep. Katherine sat there under the starlight ceiling for a few minutes. *Oh, what the hell.* She got up and headed toward the stable door.

Katherine slid the door open, giving herself only enough room to squeeze through. The only sound was the shuffling of hooves in hay––and a male snoring. Ahead of her, lying against the outer door was Gunner. Someone had cracked the door enough so he could catch the sent of any intruder––human or not. He lifted his head and gave her a look that said, *Don't worry, I've got this.* Satisfied that all was well in her new little world, Katherine stepped back and slid the door in place.

After returning to her room, Katherine tossed the quilt on the chair and crawled into bed. She'd left the bedroom door ajar to let in some of the starlight from the patio. The steady drone of the massive generator that provided life to this magical world gave her a sense of security. They were all safe enough for the night. The thought of what they might find when they returned to the real world in the morning sent a shiver through her.

23

Katherine was literally bounced awake the next morning. "Grandma, Grandma are you going to sleep all day?" The shouting along with her grandsons jumping up and down on the bed, brought her out of a sleepy fog. A quick glance around the room only caused confusion. With her brain still half asleep, she wondered just whose bed she was in. Then it all came to her in a rush. Explosions, helicopters flying overhead, hiding in the cold gorge, the mouse infested cabin——and Stuart.

"Grandma, Mrs. Russ made us breakfast! Mickey Mouse pancakes! You better get up or you'll miss it!"

"Okay, boys. How about you run along and give me a chance to get dressed."

Katherine swung her legs over the side of the bed. She sat, quietly piecing together the events of the previous day. The terror of throbbing helicopter blades still held fast in her mind.

The sound of footsteps brought Katherine's attention to the doorway. "Hey there, sleepyhead. I can't believe I'm up before you? This is a first. Guess living underground agrees with you."

"Good morning, Sylvie. I don't know what hit me. I don't remember waking at all during the night. You would think my head would have been conjuring up nightmares."

Sylvia patted her mother's knee. "Renee's whipped up a feast in that tiny kitchen and believe it or not the boys have been up for an hour."

Katherine glanced at her watch and gasped. "It can't be after seven. I've never slept this late."

Sylvia watched her mother-in-law rocket off the bed and race for her clothes. She closed the door behind her with a chuckle. Although out-of-character, it was good to know Katherine had gotten a good night's sleep. She needed it after the horrors of yesterday––they all needed it. As for the boys––it was one big adventure. One she was sure they would never forget.

It had taken Katherine just minutes to dress but already she found Sylvia and Renee chatting at the table like a couple of moms at a PTA meeting. What about the explosions and the helicopter shooting at anything that moved? Surely it hadn't just gone away, or maybe it was still out there and they would be forced to live underground like moles. Scurrying around under the protection of the night sky for food.

Renee's chair scraped the concrete floor as she scooted back and stood. "Good morning. I'll just go and get your coffee. A plate of scrambled eggs, bacon and toast will be coming up in just a minute."

"Wow! You don't need to go to all that trouble just for me. Toast will be fine."

Renee laughed. "It's already made, I just need to pop the bread in the toaster. The men haven't eaten either. Sylvia will fill you in."

The laughter coming from the playroom suddenly escalated. "Maybe I should go see how the kids are doing. It sounds like they're having too much fun. And where are the dogs?" Katherine asked.

"Don't bother. They'll barely even notice you. Renee promised them a bike ride after she's finished with breakfast. The dogs are out with Stuart and Russ."

"Will we be here that long? What's happening outside?" Katherine asked after her first sip of coffee.

"Don't know. Russ went out a couple of times during the night. He heard the helicopter off in the distance but there weren't any explosions."

"So, what's next?"

"Stuart waited until it got light then drove the golf cart to the house. He was going to make some phone calls to find out just what the status is out there and then come back."

Renee returned with a plate of steaming eggs and bacon. "Let me know if you want anything else. Jam's on the table."

Sylvia pushed a small Mason jar toward her mother-in-law. "You've got to try this. It's like heaven in a jar."

Katherine added a small amount of the red jam to her toast and took a bite. "Wow! This is amazing!"

"Strawberry and rhubarb. Renee puts it up herself."

The opening of the door to the stable stopped any further discussion of Renee's jam. Their full attention focused on Stuart and Russ.

Katherine studied the men's faces. Fresh fears of what might be waiting beyond the stable door and the safety of the shelter rushed to the surface. Stuart's easygoing gait and smile were somewhat reassuring, while Russ lagged behind with the look of a man who hadn't slept a wink all night.

Stuart eyed Katherine's plate as he approached the table. "I hope there's more of that on the stove. We're starving!"

Sylvia scooted to the side making room for two more at the table. "We heard you went to the house. What's happening out there? Will it be safe for us to leave?"

Stuart sat down across from Katherine and smiled. "I know you're worried about Michael and Morgan but you can finally relax. And I suggest you start on those eggs before they get cold. Renee doesn't take kindly to folks who don't finish a meal."

She couldn't relax. Not until she knew that Michael and Morgan were safe. She felt two sets of eyes watching her fork push the eggs across the plate. Just then Renee came through the door with two plates heaping with eggs and bacon. "Toast is on its way. But only after you give us the news. What did you find out?"

"It's all good. So, go get our toast and bring yourself a mug of coffee. It's too much to tell twice."

Katherine watched both men dig into their eggs like they hadn't eaten in a week. It was somewhat comforting to see them focused on the meal and not the horrors of yesterday. Yet, her heart raced as she reached for the jam with an unsteady hand.

Katherine braced herself as the golf cart bounced across the uneven pasture. It was the quickest way to the house and a phone. Sylvia and Renee had stayed behind to pack up while the four kids played as if living in a bomb shelter was an everyday occurrence.

Katherine grabbed one of the roof struts when the golf cart suddenly lurched forward then went airborne. Stuart reached his right arm out to steady her. Despite his assurance that her children were safe, she wouldn't relax until she wrapped her arms around them.

"Thank you for making those calls this morning to locate Michael and Morgan. I can't believe my son was actually here last night looking for us. He must have been frantic thinking we had just disappeared," Katherine said in a shaky voice.

"He left a note on both the front and back doors with his name and phone numbers––every place and number he might be for the whole day! He said The National Guard had a helicopter patrolling the area with a searchlight. It must have been the one Russ saw last night and thought it was the same one that had been circling during the day."

"Russ did say it sounded different––bigger," Katherine added.

Smoke still hung in the air and sirens gave proof that the aftermath was not yet over. Gunner led the other two dogs racing across the pasture with Saint Nick bringing up the rear.

"Michael is helping with the investigation at the old Diamond Shamrock site and the salt mine," Stuart paused while he steered the cart onto the lane leading to the house. "He'll be here as soon as he can get away. I'm sure it's a huge relief just knowing his family is safe."

Morgan's whereabouts hadn't been mentioned. That worried Katherine. Morgan should have been at the TV station following the story she was doing in the Terminal Tower. At least one of her children was safe.

Stuart brought the cart to a stop at the back door of the house. "There's a phone on the wall in the kitchen. I know you want to find Morgan so take your time. You'll find paper and pens in the desk if you need them. I'll just go and get the truck and head back to the shelter. Make yourself comfortable if Michael should come before we get back."

Katherine jumped when the kitchen door banged against the wall, a sure sign her grandsons had arrived. "Grandma, Grandma we got to ride in the back of a truck!" Nathan squealed.

Katherine had just gotten the boys settled when a second vehicle arrived. In less than a minute Michael had both his sons in his arms. Sylvia watched the happy reunion from the doorway for a few seconds before joining them for a group hug. She glanced up at her mother-in-law with tears and a smile that said her world was once again complete.

Katherine's heart filled with joy as the boys squirmed out of their father's arms and dropped to the floor.

"Daddy, Daddy! These are our two bestest friends in the whole world!" Nathan and Daniel ran over to where Renee and Russ waited with Jeremy and Emily. "We were living underground with horses! They said that we can come back this summer and swim in Mr. Royal's pool and play on their swings and get pony rides on Bella!"

Nathan and Daniel pulled Jeremy and Emily over to where Michael waited. "Can we, Dad? See, they're real nice and we really like it here!"

He squatted down to their level and glanced up at Stuart. "If it's okay with Mr. Royal, then I'm sure we can arrange something."

"I bet he'll let you and Mom come too! He and Mr. Russ are real nice," Daniel exclaimed.

Jeremy pulled on Daniel's arm. "Come on outside. We can play on the swings."

"Can we, Dad?" Daniel and Nathan jumped up and down. "Can we? Please?"

Michael ruffled his son's heads. "Sure." He watched as the four children all squeezed through the door together.

Michael stood and turned toward Katherine and Sylvia. "Maybe we should sit down at the table while I tell you about Morgan."

Both Katherine and Sylvia had panicked looks as they eased onto the chairs.

Renee poured coffee for everyone from the pot that Katherine had made earlier while she waited for Stuart's return. They all sat around the table waiting for Michael to begin.

By the time Michael finished what he knew, everyone had a pretty clear understanding of what role Morgan played in bringing down the mastermind and thieves from her discussions with the station manager, and of course Michael. He assured Katherine that Morgan had a full schedule doing location shots for the follow-up stories, so she probably wouldn't hear from her daughter until the evening. Katherine could only nod her understanding. Morgan hadn't been safe––she'd faced robbers and killers with only her microphone.

"Mom, don't worry about Morgan. I just left her doing a session at the salt mine. She interviewed me about what took place along the river. She's really amazing. That sister of mine figured this whole thing out with the help of two homeless guys!"

"I'm sure I'll get the details from her. I have a feeling we got the sugarcoated version from you." Katherine squeezed her son's hand. "I'm just glad you're both safe."

"Yeah. Well, I'd like to hear about living underground with horses. But I really need to get back. How about we take Sylvie to pick up her Explorer and she and the kids can head back to the house. I'll drop you off on my way to Fairport Harbor."

Stuart watched Katherine's expression fall from happy to dejected. The family she nearly died protecting was just going to leave her at her doorstep. This was a woman of great courage and endless love for those around her. Last night, he hadn't fallen asleep yet when he'd heard the door slide open, and the uneasy snorting and shuffling of the horses as someone entered the barn. Katherine had felt the need to check on them before she, herself, could turn in. This was not some tired old woman to send home for a nap. He'd recognized her determination and spunk from the moment he encountered her, with a wolf at her side, in his pasture. She hadn't backed down or cowered at the sight of his rifle. She was a take-charge kind of woman and he liked that, but he also recognized the soft, loving side as well. She was awakening more than protective feelings that he had long since forgotten. He couldn't just let her walk thru the door and out of his life.

"Listen, I have a better idea. Katherine can stay here and help us get things back to normal. Maybe even a hayride or two." Stuart looked at Katherine and winked. "I'll drive her home after dinner tonight." He moved to her side. "If that's okay with you?"

Katherine's smile radiated happiness. "I'd love it!" Her adventure wasn't going to end after all.

A few minutes later Stuart and Katherine stood side-by-side on the back porch, waving goodbye. Michael and family drove toward the tall gates to the estate. Russ and Renee, with the kids, drove the truck back down the farm lane toward the shelter. Lizzie and Saint Nick trotted off after the truck.

Stuart slipped his arm around Katherine's shoulder. "Come on Kate, let's finish this adventure."

24

ONE MONTH LATER

WJW-TV News station, 2:00 P.M.

M organ's tiny cubicle suddenly got smaller when Sam entered and leaned against the wall. "You'll be getting bigger digs with the promotion. I still can't believe you got an exclusive for airing the follow-up story. Do you have any idea how important national coverage is for you and the furthering of your career? You could be the next Diane Sawyer."

"I doubt that." Morgan laughed at the thought of being on nightly, national news. "Although it's both exciting and intimidating. I never thought anything this big would fall into my lap."

"How's the final segment coming?" Sam stepped away from the wall. "Not meeting the deadline isn't an option."

Morgan tapped the eraser end of her pencil on the copy she was working on. "I just wish I had the whole story. How can I have an ending without knowing the reason behind an operation that was carried out with military precision?" She shook her head. "One month *later* and I don't know where to go with *this*!" Morgan hurled the pencil against the wall of her cubicle. "It's so frustrating!"

"Calm down," Sam said in a voice meant to soothe. "The answer's out there. How about the two homeless guys that helped you?"

"They're gone––vanished. I tried to find them. When I went back with Lamar, they'd cleaned out the two rooms they were using in the tunnel and just disappeared. No one seems to have a clue where they could be."

"How about having the FBI dust for fingerprints? Sounds like they spent a lot of time in those two rooms."

Morgan swung her chair around and faced Sam. "Would you believe those rooms have been *scrubbed* with *bleach*? Even the doors!" She threw her arms up in frustration. "Who does something like that? What do they have to hide?"

"How about tracking through their last names?"

"Don't know them––no one does!" Morgan let out a loud, frustrated sigh. "Too bad. I liked them. They were good guys that didn't deserve that kind of life. What drives people to give up everything for a life on the street? I just don't understand it."

"Sounds like you're working on another possible human interest story." Sam turned to leave then glanced back. "You can call it *Life in a Box*."

"It's *not* funny, Sam," Morgan snapped back. "They're real people with real issues. Miguel's a Vietnam hero. He saved Stan's life, along with many others. He received a Purple Heart. The war messed up his head. You know, he was ready to *die* for me down there. I wish there was something I could do for him––for *them*."

"Okay, okay. I'm sorry for the crack. I'll be in my office if you need anything."

Listening to Sam's retreating steps, Morgan shook her head at his senseless remark. Maybe she should look into doing a documentary on the homeless. Their voice deserved to be heard. But at the moment she had a bigger problem at hand. Where was she going to find answers to the most important question of her career? What was in that vault? The phone calls to her cousin, Travis, had led nowhere. Although, from the tone of his voice, she was sure he had at least an inkling of what had been locked safely away in the Federal Reserve Bank. Maybe, it was still there.

Morgan's ears perked up at the sound of Sam's footsteps coming back her way. He had a distinctive gait due to a college football knee injury. It had left him with a slight limp, heavier on his right foot. They stopped at her door.

"Not finished beating up the homeless, Sam?"

He poked his head around the corner. "Someone here to see you. Said he knows you from the tunnels."

"Funny, Sam. Next, you're going to tell me you put a homeless guy in the conference room."

"This guy is far from homeless. His watch cost more than I make in a year."

"Don't know anyone that fits that description. How about you handle it. I've got phone calls to make."

"Said he has the information you've been looking for. What the hell have you got to lose, Morgan? Anything new that *he* might have is better than *your* nothing."

Morgan pushed back her chair and stood. "You win, Sam. I'll go check out this tunnel buddy."

Morgan hesitated at the door before entering the conference room. Sam should have added a custom-tailored suit that hugged a tall, trim body. His expertly cut sandy-colored hair stopped just above a starched, white shirt collar. He stood at the windows gazing out at what she knew to be the unattractive view of the parking lot. He flexed his shoulders. There were muscles under the charcoal-gray silk suit jacket. Her mind searched its databank. Nothing about this man matched anyone she'd met in the tunnels––at least not his back. Maybe the insufferable FBI agent? What was his name? McGuire–– no, he wore polyester.

Morgan cleared her throat. "I was told you wanted to speak with me."

He turned slowly, deliberately. Was he challenging her to iden- tify him? The shine on his shoes caught her attention––expensive–– maybe Italian. She'd seen a similar pair while doing a piece on a new men's clothing store that had opened in the Galleria the year before.

Yeah, those shoes were definitely Italian. Her gaze followed trousers with a sharp crease up past a well-manicured hand peeking out from a starched cuff adorned with a gold and onyx link. A discreet, gray-striped tie nestled between the lapels of a beautifully cut jacket. His skin was smooth. Perhaps a little more tan than would be expected in May. Did he have a job that kept him outdoors? Then her eyes locked with his. Sultry, gray—no, they were blue. Only one person had those eyes.

It couldn't be. A cold chill numbed her senses, threatening to freeze her mind. She'd never fainted before, but suddenly Morgan knew what it felt like, just before her body went limp. She took several deep breaths to push down the fog and grabbed the door jam.

Stan reached her in three strides. Taking her free arm, he kicked the door closed behind them and guided her toward the table.

"Sorry, Morgan. I didn't mean to shock you like this. You looked like you'd seen a ghost." Stan eased her into a chair then poured a glass of water from a pitcher on the table. He placed it in her hand.

Morgan's brain pushed its way through the fog. "I tried to find you and Miguel. No one knew where you'd gone." She took a deep, steadying breath. "I was worried about you. I wanted to help you. Maybe find you a place to live."

She took a sip while studying his suit—expensive—real expensive. Feelings of hurt and anger pushed through the fog to the surface. He'd deliberately deceived her. Lied to her. "You obviously don't need my help."

Stan sat on the edge of the table facing Morgan. "I'd mentioned to you while we were sitting in the plaza that I'd been trying to get help for Miguel, but he wasn't ready. Well, that whole episode with you really jump-started Miguel's emotions into high gear. He became focused and was not just following directions, he was thinking on his own. The tunnels were crawling with police, FBI and agents from the Treasury. We spent the next week under a bridge. Miguel couldn't handle the inactivity. We managed to get everything out of the *toy box* before the rest of the tunnels were searched. It's safe now and only I have access to it. I was able to get Miguel into a program with the VA in Washington. He's doing remarkably well."

Morgan set the glass on the table with enough force to slosh the liquid. "But that still doesn't explain the *man* standing before me. You *lied* to me! Just who the hell are you?"

Stan stood and took a few purposeful steps back to the windows. He leaned against the sill, taking his time before answering. "What you see is really the old me. The man I was before I took on the responsibility of Miguel. He saved my life in that God forsaken country. I couldn't stand by and watch him spend the rest of his days under a bridge or in a tunnel, as it were."

"But you *lied* to me!" Morgan reached a hand up to stroke a throbbing temple. "I *believed* you! I *trusted* you! I wanted to *help* you."

Stan took a step forward.

Morgan motioned for him to stop. "*Don't* come near me! I don't know who the hell you are or what game you're playing!"

He took a deep breath. "My name is Stanley Royal."

Morgan felt her brow crease. Her mother was always telling her not to frown or she would get ugly lines before her time. She was doing it now, and it was her mother who'd introduced her to Stuart Royal. They were seeing quite a lot of each other and Morgan had heard more than a few stories about the well-decorated Stanley. He was Stuart's only son, and heir to the paint dynasty. He was off somewhere doing his own thing to help a war buddy. She'd never made the connection, not even when Stuart proudly showed her the framed photos that decorated his library of the incredibly handsome Stanley. Her Stan had long hair and a full beard. Like he'd just come down from the hills of Tennessee, with a little bit of change in his pocket.

Morgan wasn't ready to trust this new Stan or Stanley, even if her heart was beginning to thaw––her mind was still in control. He'd invaded her thoughts far too often in the past month. She'd admired the man whose strength and willingness to put his life on the line for a stranger was only shadowed by hypnotic blue eyes and a voice that sent chills up her spine. He was rough on the outside and gentle on the inside. But that man didn't exist. He hadn't trusted her enough to tell her the truth. Could she trust him now? She'd better keep the conversation professional.

Morgan grasped the glass, as much for some sort of emotional support, as any intention to drink. "Sam said something about having some answers for me," she said with a matter-of-fact edge to her voice.

Stan couldn't take his eyes off of the woman who had reigned over his mind for the past month. The courageous woman who wouldn't leave his thoughts and now he realized she had also taken control of his heart. He'd wanted her to see him as he really was, someone successful, someone she could admire. Stan wanted to be someone worthy, not a homeless bum to feel ashamed of——to pity. He'd tracked down Morgan and Michael's cousin, Travis Tanner, at his estate, Fairfield, after admitting Miguel to the VA hospital in Virginia. They'd hit it off right from the start. They both anticipated Morgan's excitement when she heard the story behind the Federal Reserve Bank's secret deposit. He'd been so worried about making a good impression that it never occurred to him that she might take his appearance in a negative way. The death-grip she had on the glass said volumes. He needed to move slowly. She was ready to walk out of the room and out of his life forever. Stan knew the only thing that would hold her here was the story.

He moved to the opposite chair and sat down, keeping the safe space of the conference table between them. "Look, Morgan, I know this is a shock. But as much as I wanted to tell you who I am and why I was there, I couldn't. I was living that life for Miguel, it was his story——and you're a reporter."

"Yeah, I get it," Morgan said with anger and hurt in her voice. "And I suppose you and Miguel living in the tunnels wasn't some clandestine operation——the steam company gave you the keycards."

"I'm a Board member. But they don't know about the *toy box*," Stan said with a bit of humor.

"Great. I feel like a fool. I fell for the whole charade." Morgan's chest heaved with a sigh that deflated her whole body.

"Look, I didn't want to leave you like that. But under the circumstances, I didn't have a choice. I *did* stay in the shadows and watch—just in case you needed me."

Morgan nodded. "I saw your hunched form in the doorway across the street from the loading dock." She swallowed. "I wanted to wave. To give you some sign that I knew you were there." She blinked back tears threatening to spill forth. "I knew in my heart you were there for me, watching over me, not to view the circus unfolding on the street." Morgan sniffled. "I gave my viewers a rundown on all the activity, the various agencies blocking the street, law enforcement officers escorting prisoners in handcuffs to waiting vehicles—lights flashing—pandemonium. When I looked back, you were gone."

"I couldn't take the chance that some sharp-eyed officer would see me and want a statement. Once I knew you had everything under control I took off." He paused as if remembering something. "One thing puzzled me at the time—still does. I counted a total of fifteen guys being arrested. That's a hell of a lot of manpower to pull off one heist. And fifteen ways to split the loot?" Stan shrugged. "Doesn't make sense, even with what I know now."

Morgan glanced up, but her eyes didn't go any further than the knot of Stan's gray-striped tie. But still, her pulse raced. "Wasn't going to be a split," she paused to slow her breathing. "After everyone left, the head agent with the FBI ordered that the ambulances be moved to one of their lots for examination. The two had just cleared the entrance ramp onto I90 when they both exploded, killing the drivers."

"I watched all of your interviews and coverage, that part was never mentioned."

"It won't be until the final segment." Morgan felt warm inside—he'd watched her interviews. "Once all those guys were told about their planned deaths, they started singing like a jail full of canaries."

"Huh." There was a lot more to the story than he and Travis had learned from their meetings with Nicholas Brady, the Secretary of the Treasury. Apparently while he was busy in Washington following the loot, Morgan was busy in Cleveland with the FBI following the heist. Better tell her how he'd been working with Travis this past month or she'd *really* be pissed.

"Turns out they were all hired independently to do a specific job. They knew it was for something big––but not what. The guys in the jeeps, over a month's time, had placed explosive devices in abandoned or unused buildings, making sure each would make a big enough bang to keep the authorities busy and assuming the Perry nuclear plant was next. On that Sunday, they drove to those locations and detonated the bombs electronically. The helicopter pilot took out the more remote locations, while creating additional terror on the ground."

"So, the machine gun operators on the back of the jeeps were just for show?"

"No. They were for real. And would have been used if necessary–– like the poor guys near the salt mine who were killed."

Stan and Morgan spent the next couple minutes in silence, each wondering how much more to tell the other. One thing Stan knew for sure––he had to confess about Travis.

"Morgan, going back to when you last saw me. I knew there was nothing more I could do for you. I had to protect Miguel and me, and our life on the streets. It took us a week to clear out and when he finally announced that he wanted to get help, I jumped on it. I arranged for Miguel to undergo inpatient treatment at a VA hospital in Virginia. I remembered you mentioning your cousin, Travis Tanner, and his connections in Washington. So, after getting Miguel settled at the VA hospital, I gave Travis a call. We met a few times. He's a great guy and speaks very highly of you. He pulled some strings and we got the whole story on what those goons were after. The Federal Reserve and the Treasury Department are giving you an exclusive on the story."

Morgan looked into Stan's eyes for the first time since he began his story. She savored the warmth of his smile. "Thank you for seeing this through. I wasn't getting anywhere, not even with Travis––now I know why."

Stan nodded in understanding. "I'm sure he wouldn't have helped me if it weren't for a few mutual friends in high places. We worked together on this. It's quite an amazing story."

He pushed his chair back and stood, then moved toward the window. His movement sent a hint of some soft and very sensual cologne drifting in her direction. She hadn't meant to take a deep breath, it just happened, filling her lungs with a scent that awakened erotic feelings she desperately tried to ignore.

Stan smiled his Cheshire cat smile. It was that knowing smile she remembered from the tunnels. The smile that said he knew what she was thinking. But he couldn't know, she didn't even know––not really.

"Of course, it will mean a trip to Washington to actually see the loot."

"My exclusive includes filming what the thieves were after?" The last vestiges of anger quickly washed away with thoughts of a Pulitzer.

"Yes." Stan's laugh was soft and sensual, at least to Morgan's ears it was, sending a shiver of excitement through her. "Whenever you're ready," he finished.

Morgan took a sip of water. Stan could see the wheels turning in her head. She was hooked. He waited for her reply. "Okay, what's the story?"

Stan unbuttoned his suit jacket and put both hands into his trouser pockets. He leaned back against the windowsill, crossing his legs at the ankles. He oozed sex appeal, wealth and casual confidence in both himself and his place in the world. A picture of a man who could grace the cover of Forbes––perhaps he had.

His mouth inched up at the corner. Once again, he knew what she was thinking. How maddening, Morgan thought.

"It all started back in 1881 when silver was discovered near what is now Barstow, California. A small mining town emerged named Calico. It wasn't actually all that small due to the King Mine which was the largest silver mine in California. Imagine––the town had a weekly newspaper, three hotels, five general stores, a meat market, bars, brothels and three restaurants and boarding houses. Along with doctors, lawyers and schools, it had a Wells Fargo office––in 1881."

"Okay, so it was King Silver Mine money that our guys were after?" Morgan asked.

"No. Harvey Pinter and Horace Hill were two prospectors who were working a small mine that played out about the time that the mines around Calico were at their peak. Between 1883 and 1885, Calico had over 500 mines in operation and a population of 1,200. Harvey and Horace pulled-up stakes and started a new mine in the area, the H & H Silver Mine. They did very well, and H & H Silver was making quite a name for itself when in 1885 Harvey was gunned down on his way home for the silver in his pocket."

Stan paused and walked back to the table and poured himself a glass of water.

He took a sip and continued. "You might say that Horace began to see the writing on the wall. Notoriety may not be all that good. So, he took the money they had in the Wells Fargo bank and started a cattle ranch on the land that had been his first mine. A barn was built over the entrance to the mineshaft and during the next eight years Horace moved the silver he mined to the ranch and stored it under the barn, in the old mine shaft. It's estimated that he moved over a million dollars in silver before the repeal of the Sherman Silver Purchase Act in 1893 which ended the silver boom."

Morgan sifted through this news as any reporter would, attempting to tie California history to present-day Cleveland. "Too bad for the silver market, but how does that fast forward to today?"

"By now Horace was losing faith in the United States government along with life as a prospector in Calico. He closed the played-out mine and focused on cattle."

Stan took another sip of water and smiled.

"Turns out that back in 1891 old Horace was alone and angry with California and the lawless world at the time. Having no family, he didn't want anyone else to profit from his hard work. He didn't have much faith in the federal government, which he saw as corrupt. So, he worked out a new will with his attorney and executed it through the Wells Fargo Bank."

Morgan was now seeing a method to old Horace's thinking. "Don't stop now, what did he do?"

"Horace figured it would take a hundred years for the government to get its shit together and be able to put his money to good use. So, on April 22, 1991, Horace's land and everything under it became the property of the United States of America."

Morgan did the math in her head and came up with a problem. "So, on April 21st the silver should have still been safe under the barn in California . . . I don't get it."

"There was an earthquake that damaged the mineshaft. The officials at Wells Fargo, who had been managing the land all those years, decided the silver needed to be moved to a safe location and held until the government took possession on the 22nd."

"And they picked *Cleveland*?"

Stan chuckled. "It worked, didn't it?"

"So, it was raw silver ore they were after. Now I understand the need for large canvas bags and motorized carts. That ore had to weigh a ton! But could it possibly be valuable enough to warrant such an elaborate operation?"

"That silver could fund a small country for a very long time."

Morgan watched Stan's right eyebrow raise and the smile that turned into a grin. She knew that look well. He was on to something. God, she had missed that look––the look that could send a rush of adrenaline pushing her forward.

Stan moved to the edge of the table sitting with one leg draped over the corner. "The big question is. Who found out about the transfer and had the ability to organize an operation of that size?"

Morgan took advantage of his closeness to inhale deeply. He smelled sooo good! She pushed back all the sensual feelings begging to take over and considered Stan's last words. Now, the lack of knowledge, at the time Mr. Gruff was interviewed by the FBI made sense. Stan and Morgan had fingered him as the ringleader, the one calling the shots. But he was only the Cleveland crew's handler. He too was expendable. "We only caught the guys hired to steel the silver––not the brains behind it."

"I remember something that I thought odd while I was watching the loading dock. Think back to the last time we were huddled together listening to the goons' voices? Another guy showed up. He sounded older, more educated than the others. I didn't see anyone being arrested that was older."

"I remember," Morgan said. "After hours of reviewing the filming with the FBI. I noticed a distinguished-looking man with gray hair. He was in the tunnel when we first turned on the lights. We got everyone's face except his. Then, on the loading dock we covered the whole takedown with the police and FBI––he's not in any of the frames."

Stan didn't answer for a few moments. "So, he was in the tunnel while the plastic was being put around the door. If I remember correctly, he advised them to stop. Then Lamar hit the lights and you began speaking. The officers charged in and herded everyone out to the loading dock where they were arrested and hauled off."

"Right, but gray-haired man isn't one of them. Jerry and I both think he found a hidey-hole in the basement and waited until all was quiet."

"He could be the local organizer and knew he would be the only one still alive by the end of the day," Stan shook his head. "Hold on. What about the silver? They weren't putting it in the ambulances–– not enough room and especially if the plan was to blow them up."

"We figured that out as well. There was a large box truck, parked in the construction site next door. One of the agents noticed that the gate's lock was broken and investigated. From the outside, it looked like the truck contained plumbing supplies for the Bank One job. However, it turned out to be empty. It had one of those elevator-type platforms on the back. A phone call to the construction company the next morning confirmed our suspicions that the truck didn't belong to their plumbing supplier. The advertising on both sides of the truck turned out to be large plastic sheets that peeled off. We guess that at some point Mr. gray-haired man would remove the plumbing company's graphics and continue on his route in a plain white truck."

"So, the silver was going to be loaded into an innocent-looking delivery truck. Maybe with the gray-haired man driving––brilliant." Stan slapped his knee.

"It *was* brilliant, and I'm guessing took at least a year to plan," Morgan added.

"Yep, and every government agency is working the details. You'll hear about it as soon as it's released for your story."

"Any ideas of who could have pulled it off?"

Stan hopped off the corner of the table. "I'm betting on someone at the Wells Fargo office in California, maybe even the attorney handling the transfer."

Morgan pushed her chair back. She stood before the man who sent chills racing through her body.

"Well, Stanley Royal, does this mean we're going to finish this story together?"

"I certainly hope so." Stan took her in his arms. His kiss brought forth every emotion he'd felt since she'd barged into his life and every fantasy he'd had since leaving her.

The touch of Stan's lips, the hunger in his kiss sent Morgan into another dimension, one of erotic sensations, mental excitement–– and love.

AUTHOR BIO

Pamela Ann Cleverly is a novelist and member of Romance Writers of America and Sisters in Crime. She lives in northeastern Ohio where she is finishing her forth book; a paranormal titled *A Paper Key*.

Pamela is the Executive Director for CANTER Ohio, a non-profit organization dedicated to providing Thoroughbred ex-racehorses the opportunity for a new life, home and career through rehabilitation, retraining and rehoming. She is also the Co-Executive Director for CANTER Kentucky.

www.ingramcontent.com/pod-product-compliance
Lightning Source LLC
Chambersburg PA
CBHW051259250626
47155CB00009B/3359